Happy 25th birthday, Harlequin Presents,

May the next 25 years be as much fun!

Love, as always,

Carole Mortimer

Dear Reader,

Like you, I'm thrilled and excited to see Harlequin
Presents®' twenty-fifth anniversary. The year 1998
marks my eighteenth year of writing for Presents.
During that time I have written almost one hundred
books for the line—and I've enjoyed writing, and
being part of, every single one of them! Love and
romance are what keep my world turning, as I'm sure
they do yours; and having someone of your own to
love, that special someone, makes life all the more
satisfying and exciting. Harlequin Presents® stories
give the same glow—long may they continue!

Love, as always,

Carole Mortimer

Carole Mortimer

CAROLE MORTIMER

The Diamond Bride

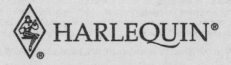

HARLEQUIN®

TORONTO • NEW YORK • LONDON
AMSTERDAM • PARIS • SYDNEY • HAMBURG
STOCKHOLM • ATHENS • TOKYO • MILAN • MADRID
PRAGUE • WARSAW • BUDAPEST • AUCKLAND

For Tim

ISBN 0-373-11966-6

THE DIAMOND BRIDE

First North American Publication 1998.

CHAPTER ONE

'IF YOU'RE thinking of jumping, I should wait another couple of hours until the tide is back in!'

Annie turned with a start at the sound of that deeply masculine voice—a voice she didn't recognise!

A dark figure loomed in the fog. A tall, menacing figure.

'At the moment,' that deep voice continued, 'you'll most likely just find yourself buried up to your ankles in mud!'

She had been lost in thought as she stood on the end of this small jetty, troubled thoughts that went round and round in circles, their beginnings always meeting up with their ends, giving no answers.

She had been so lost in those thoughts she hadn't heard the man's approach, but she was conscious now of how alone she was, the thick, swirling afternoon fog meaning she couldn't be seen by anyone up at the house that stood so majestically on the clifftop above. This small, private beach was rarely used by any member of the Diamond family, and was certainly not going to be visited by any of them at this time of the day.

Alone now, with this stranger, she realised how foolish her choice had been.

'I also don't think the Diamond family would be too pleased at another suicide taking place on their estate,' the gravelly voice continued harshly.

Another suicide…? Had someone once killed themselves here? What—?

Another suicide! Surely this man didn't imagine that was what she intended doing down here? Although in truth, with the tide obviously out, and the fog making visibility negligible, it must seem strange for her to be standing out here on this waterless jetty. But suicide…!

She took an involuntary step backwards as the man moved towards her out of the mist, only to find herself pressed up against the railing with nowhere to go—except, as he'd said, down into the mud below.

Her eyes widened apprehensively as the fog seemed to part to allow the man to step out in front of her—a man, she was sure, who must be the epitome of every fictional hero.

She gasped even as the ridiculous thought jumped into her head. But at first sight he was the personification of that romantic hero Rochester: so tall, dark hair long and unruly, his face strong and powerful, eyes as dark as coal. He was Rochester come to life!

Annie shivered. Whether because of this overpowering stranger, or the dampness of the fog penetrating to her bones through the light jacket and denims she wore, she wasn't altogether sure.

'Cat got your tongue?' he challenged with a rise of one dark brow.

Up close—too close!—she could see that his eyes weren't black at all, but a very deep blue, the iris barely discernible from that dark cobalt, his features so hardly hewn they might have been carved from granite.

He tilted his head to one side, his expression speculative, black hair resting almost on his shoulders, seem-

ing immune himself to the dampness of the weather in
his dark jacket, blue casual shirt and faded blue denims.

'"Trespassers will be prosecuted"'. He dryly quoted
the sign that precluded access onto this secluded beach.

She swallowed hard, moistening her lips as she realised how dry her mouth had become. But the only way
off the jetty was past this man, and being slightly
built—only a little over five feet in height—she thought
her chances of making good her escape were probably
a little slim.

An avid reader, she tried to think what a fictional her-
oine would do in these circumstances. Humour him, that
was it. Then wait until he was off-guard—and make a
run for it. Once she had disappeared into the thick fog
he would have great trouble finding her again.

She attempted a slight, conciliatory smile. 'I'm sure
that if you leave now the Diamond family will never be
aware that you were ever here at all,' she suggested
lightly—desperately hoping that none of the panic she
felt was evident in her voice.

Dark eyes widened. 'If I leave…?' He frowned. 'My
dear girl, I have no intention of leaving.'

He didn't intend leaving…

Annie swallowed hard again, hands tightly clenched
in her jacket pockets. 'I really think that would be the
best thing for you to do.' She forced soothing calm into
her voice. 'Before—er—Mr Diamond comes down here
and finds you trespassing on his land.'

'Mr Diamond…?' he echoed questioningly.

'Anthony Diamond,' Annie supplied quickly, at last
feeling she might be making some progress in her effort
to get him to leave.

'He's here?' the man rasped, casting a look in the

direction of the house above on the cliff, now hidden by the fog.

'Oh, yes.' She nodded eagerly. 'All of the family are in residence.'

'Are they indeed?' he mused harshly, his brow clearing, his mouth twisting with contempt. 'Well, I can assure you there's no possibility of Anthony coming down here,' he dismissed derisively. 'He hates the sea and everything to do with it—more so since a boating accident several years ago. Unless, of course, the two of you have arranged to meet down here?' he added slowly.

Annie looked at him sharply, momentarily forgetting her fear. Exactly what did he mean by that remark? He couldn't possibly know anything about Anthony—or her, for that matter.

'Have you?' he prompted softly. 'It would be the one place Davina wouldn't think of looking for him; she knows of his aversion to moving water!' he mocked.

And this man, she realised, at the mention of Davina, Anthony's fiancée—whoever he was—knew far too much about the Diamond family!

The man looked at her consideringly now, seeming to take in everything about her appearance in that one sweeping glance: her short, curling red hair, which framed her gamine face, a face dominated by deep brown eyes; her small and snub nose, her wide and smiling mouth—usually, when she wasn't accosted by complete strangers!—a chin that was small and pointed, her figure boyish in her jacket, blue cropped top and fitted black denims.

'You don't look like Anthony's usual type,' the man finally drawled insultingly. 'But then, as he gets older, perhaps young and impressionable is easier to deal with!'

Easier to impress, his dismissive tone implied!

Well, at thirty-six, she didn't consider Anthony old, and she wasn't that young either; at twenty-two she could quite easily be married with small children.

She eyed the man coolly. 'Anthony Diamond, as you have already mentioned, already has a fiancée.' Some of her fear was fading now, to be replaced by anger; not only was this man trespassing on the Diamond estate, he was also insulting the family—well, one of them—as well now!

'Davina,' the man acknowledged. 'I'm sure their engagement is of mutual benefit to both of them,' he went on, 'but it hasn't stopped Anthony's roving eye. You must be new to the village,' he added tauntingly. 'Last I heard, Anthony had already gone through all the available females there. Unless, of course, you're one of the married ones?'

It had quickly become obvious to her that this man thought she was one of the girls from the local village two miles away. Which meant he must be new to the area himself, otherwise he would have known she was nanny to the youngest member of the Diamond family. Admittedly, she had only been working here for two months, but he seemed to know so much else about the Diamonds...

'I'm not married, but I'm not an "available female", either,' Annie told him tartly. 'And I would appreciate it if you didn't continue to insult members of the Diamond family!'

'But I'm only insulting Anthony,' he replied knowingly. 'And he makes it so easy to insult him,' he added scathingly, glancing at the plain gold watch on his wrist. 'It doesn't look as if he's coming now; I was watching you for at least ten minutes before I spoke to you,' he informed her softly.

She shrank back defensively, uncomfortable with the knowledge that she had been watched when she hadn't been aware of it. Her emotions had been in turmoil when she'd come down here, her thoughts troubled, and she was sure that must have been obvious from her expression when he'd first caught sight of her. Which was probably why he had made that assumption about suicide! Admittedly, her life did feel a bit complicated at the moment, but certainly not that desperate!

'Perhaps it's as well that he didn't. For your sake,' she snapped as he raised questioning brows. 'You're trespassing,' she pointed out irritably as he still looked unimpressed.

He shrugged unconcernedly. 'So are you. And although Anthony may not mind your being here, what about the rest of the family?' he challenged. 'Rufus, for example?'

'Rufus isn't here,' she told him impatiently, tired of this constant baiting.

Rufus Diamond, the male head of the family and her small charge's father, was away at the moment, and had been for the last three months. As an investigative reporter of some repute, he had been away in some war-torn country or other since before Annie had come to work with his daughter. His mother, Celia, the matriarch of the Diamond family, had been the one to employ her when the previous nanny had left without notice.

The man looked at her assessingly. 'I thought you said

all of the family were in residence?' He tauntingly echoed her words of earlier.

'They are.' She frowned at him. 'But Mr Diamond
senior—'

'You mean Rufus?' Amusement darkened his eyes
even more; his teeth were white and even as he gave a
wolfish grin. 'I've never heard him referred to as that
before; you make him sound ancient!'

'I have no idea how old Mr Diamond—Mr Rufus
Diamond—is,' Annie told him in a flustered voice. 'But
I do know he's older than Anthony.'

'By three years.' The man nodded. 'And, believe me,
I feel every one of them,' he added, watching her as he
waited for her reaction to his announcement.

And he wasn't disappointed, Annie felt sure!

This was Rufus Diamond? This man, with his shag-
gily long dark hair, piercing eyes, hard-hewn face, tall
and leanly powerful body? This was Rufus Diamond?

She didn't know what she had been expecting from
the brief mentions of him that had been made by the rest
of the family, or from the absolute adoration with which
Jessica spoke of her father, but it certainly hadn't been
this dangerously good-looking man with his assured air
of power!

Perhaps it was that he was such a complete contrast
to his brother; Anthony was tall and blond, extremely
handsome, with eyes as blue as the sky on a summer's
day, always immaculately dressed in his tailored, de-
signer clothes. The two men were complete opposites,
and she would never have guessed they were brothers.

She hadn't!

She drew in a controlling breath, doing her best to
gather her scattered wits back together. 'It's good to

meet you at last, Mr Diamond.' She held out her hand in formal greeting.

He didn't move, watching her through narrowed lids. 'Is it?' he returned guardedly.

She swallowed hard, her arm falling back to her side, her hands feeling slightly warm and damp, despite the cold clamminess of the fog that still surrounded them. 'I'm Jessica's new nanny, Mr Diamond—'

'Are you indeed?' he cut in grimly, all humour gone from those hard dark eyes now. 'What about Margaret?'

She moistened her dry lips once more, some of her earlier fear returning; this man was a power to be reckoned with when he was angry. As he was now. 'I believe she left—'

'I've already gathered that,' he rasped icily.

'Yes, well.' Annie looked confused. 'Mrs Diamond contacted the employment agency—'

'Why?' His grimness was increasing with each passing second.

Annie frowned. 'I just told you, Margaret left, and Jessica needed—'

'I meant, why did Margaret leave?' he bit out coldly.

'I have no idea.' She shook her head a little dazedly. 'You would have to ask Mrs Diamond that—'

'Don't worry, that's exactly what I'm here to do!' he replied harshly, turning on his heel and striding off down the jetty in the direction of the cliffs and the house. He paused before the fog swallowed him up completely, turning slightly. 'And I would advise you to get back to your young charge instead of mooning about down here waiting for my wastrel of a brother!' He disappeared into the swirling clouds, and everything suddenly became eerily quiet again.

As if he had never been there at all...

But Annie knew that he had, was still shaking from the encounter. She almost wished now that he had been a trespasser; that would have been far preferable to knowing he was actually her employer!

How quickly his mocking humour had vanished once he'd realised exactly who she was. He was obviously very angry at the departure of Jessica's previous nanny. And certainly not impressed with her replacement!

Rochester, indeed! She had read the classic story at a young, impressionable age, had found herself, probably because of her own parentless circumstances, relating to Jane Eyre, although her own time as an orphan in care had been a relatively happy one. But Rufus Diamond certainly wasn't Mr Rochester. Any more than she was Jane Eyre...!

Would she have behaved any differently if she had known who he was from the first? Probably, but only slightly, she conceded. After all, he had been the one, without knowing a thing about her, who'd been so in-sulting about her supposed relationship with his brother...

Her thoughts were even more troubled now than they had been when she'd come down onto the beach an hour ago! She had been so excited about the chance of this job on the east coast of England, had come here full of enthusiasm, glad to be out of London, the place she had lived all her life. And being out here, surrounded by rural countryside, had suited her perfectly. She loved the wide open spaces, the friendliness of the locals—she had cer-tainly never been on a first-name basis with a milkman before! In London she hadn't even had a milkman; she had bought all her food supplies, including milk, from a convenience store around the corner from the flat she'd shared with three other girls.

Moving here had offered her a completely different way of life from the one she had always known. Her early years had been spent in care, and the college course to qualify as a children's nanny had seemed the obvious choice of career after years of helping look after younger children at the home where she had been placed. As had deciding to share a flat with three of the other girls from the children's home when the time had come to move out.

She had taken employment at a local kindergarten once she was qualified, but helping in the day-care of forty young children who went home to their own families at the end of each day hadn't given her any more roots than she had found at the children's home, and so she had signed on at an employment agency with the intention of working in a family environment. Jessica Diamond was her first individual charge. And Annie had quickly learnt to love her.

Aged eight, Jessica was a lovely child, tall for her age, with long, curling dark hair and eyes as blue as cornflowers, and a lively intelligence that Annie found enchanting. And with only Jessica's grandmother in residence most of the time, her uncle Anthony a regular visitor at weekends, it had been easy to become fond of the little girl who greeted her so eagerly at the end of each schoolday. Their weekends had been spent exploring the beach and horse-riding; even wet days had been fun as they'd played with the numerous toys Jessica had up in her bedroom.

But now Jessica's father had returned.

And he didn't seem at all happy about the fact that his daughter had a new nanny...

The future suddenly looked even bleaker than it had an hour ago. Even more so because once Rufus Diamond got up to the house he was going to discover that Jessica had fallen from her horse over the weekend and was resting in bed with a badly sprained ankle. So much for being in the care of her newly hired nanny!

Admittedly, there had been nothing Annie—a mere novice when it came to riding a horse—could have done to prevent Jessica's accident. But she very much doubted that Rufus Diamond would see it quite that way, especially as he already seemed so displeased at Jessica having a replacement nanny in the first place!

Annie felt the prick of tears in her eyes. She had loved Jessica on sight, their better acquaintance only deepening that emotion as she'd discovered just how hungry for affection Jessica was too. Perhaps she shouldn't have let Jessica become that fond of her, but when the young child was effectively as parentless as Annie had been herself, it was impossible to push the young girl aside.

As Jessica's mother had died when Jessica was still a very young child, she really had little memory of her. Celia Diamond, Jessica's paternal grandmother, was a tall, stately-looking woman, blonde and still beautiful despite her sixty-or-so years, but a woman who obviously found it difficult to show affection to a young child; a summons to her private sitting-room before bedtime was the most attention she paid her granddaughter.

But Jessica's father was back now, so perhaps things would change...

And one of those changes could be the dismissal of the new nanny!

Annie's feet dragged with reluctance as she made her way back up to the house. Nevertheless she took the path carefully—the weather seemed to be worse than when she had set out and she grabbed onto the handrail several times as she almost lost her footing on the rocky path, relieved when she saw the ominous shape of the house rising up in front of her.

Clifftop House was a magnificent building, almost gothic in proportions, and it had taken Annie a week to find her way around its many rooms. It had seemed incredible to her at the time of her arrival that one elderly lady and a small child should live in such a large house.

Although she had to admit that within several hours of Anthony's arrival at the weekend, with his fiancée, for a week's visit, the house hadn't seemed big enough for all of them!

She had a feeling it was going to seem even less so with Rufus Diamonds's impressive presence!

'Really, Rufus, I didn't see the point in contacting you,' Celia Diamond was protesting impatiently as Annie moved quietly past the sitting-room doorway. 'The doctor said it's a simple sprain, nothing to get in a panic about, and Annie has been taking very good care of her—'

'Who the hell is Annie?' that oh, so familiar voice rasped harshly.

'The new nanny you seem so angry about,' Celia responded coldly. 'You weren't here, Rufus—but then, you never are,' she added cuttingly. 'What else was I supposed to do when Margaret walked out so unexpectedly?'

Annie couldn't move, had become frozen to the spot the moment she heard her name mentioned...!

'I suppose it was too much to expect that you could look after Jessica yourself,' Rufus drawled scathingly. 'Although you still haven't given me an acceptable explanation as to exactly why Margaret walked out. And if this Annie is taking such good care of Jess, why is it that she's upstairs in bed at this moment with a leg injury?'

Annie gasped at the injustice of this last remark; there was simply no way, without completely smothering the child, that she could monitor every move of her young charge. And Jessica had been riding for years; in fact, this man had bought her the horse she had fallen from!

'Maybe I should just ask Annie that myself!' Even as Rufus spoke, the door to the sitting-room was wrenched completely open, exposing an embarrassed Annie eavesdropping in the hallway. 'Well?' Rufus Diamond barked at her. 'I presume you are Annie?'

She looked at him with widely startled eyes—and it wasn't all due to being caught out in this way. He knew damn well she was Annie; she had told him down at the jetty that she was his daughter's nanny.

'Really, Rufus,' Celia Diamond admonished haughtily. 'Sometimes I find it difficult to believe you could possibly be David's son; he was always such a gentleman, so aware of his position as head of this family,' she continued scathingly.

Rufus gave her a contemptuous glance. 'You mean you were always so aware of your position as wife of the head of this family!' he returned disgustedly. 'I'm sure my father only died at the relatively early age of sixty-five so that he could at last get away from you and your social-climbing!'

'Really, Rufus!' Celia's gasp was one of dismay now

as she clutched at the double string of pearls about her throat, her expression one of deep hurt. 'Your long absence hasn't made your tongue any kinder. And have you forgotten there are servants present?' She flicked a chilling look in Annie's direction.

She meant her, Annie realised after several stunned moments. A servant! Well…she supposed she was, in a way; she did work for these people, and was paid a wage for doing so. But even so…!

'I don't think Annie took too kindly to that last remark, Celia,' Rufus Diamond interjected.

Annie turned her gaze in his direction, only to find those dark eyes regarding her with amusement. He had obviously been watching her every expression—and deriving great enjoyment from doing so!

Her head went back proudly. 'Mrs Diamond is perfectly correct in her statement,' she said smoothly. 'This appears to be an extremely private family conversation. But I would be quite happy, Mr Diamond, to talk to you about Jessica's accident at a more convenient time.' She met his eyes challengingly, still slightly confused as to why he didn't seem to have told his mother that the two of them had already met earlier down on the beach.

Why hadn't he told Celia Diamond? Why hadn't she confessed? The answer to the last was easy; she shouldn't really have been down on the beach at all this afternoon. Celia Diamond had warned her when she'd first come to work here not to go down there when the weather was like it was today…

'Now is a convenient time for me,' Rufus Diamond invited her.

'It's Annie's afternoon off,' Celia told him quickly before Annie could make any sort of reply.

Rufus looked at her with narrowed eyes now. 'Is it indeed?' he finally drawled slowly.

Annie didn't need to be told that, with this new information, he was again adding up two and two and coming up with the answer of five! The speculation was clearly there in his mocking gaze.

'It is,' she confirmed briskly. 'But I'm not going anywhere, except upstairs to check on Jessica, so I'll be perfectly happy to talk to you once you've finished your conversation with your mother—' She broke off with a puzzled frown as her remark brought forth a harsh laugh from Rufus. 'Did I say something…funny?' she said haltingly—although for the life of her she couldn't imagine what it had been.

'To me, yes. To Celia, no,' Rufus replied, his grin wolfish again now, as it had been down on the beach. 'If you've been here two months someone really should have filled you in on the family history by now—'

'Rufus!' Celia admonished sharply, two spots of angry colour in her cheeks.

He gave her only a cursory glance. 'Something else the servants shouldn't know?' he taunted.

Celia gave him one of her chilling looks—a look that had no visible effect on him whatsoever!—before turning back to Annie. 'Perhaps if you wouldn't mind going and checking on Jessica now…?' she suggested smoothly—although it was more in the order of an instruction. 'I'm sure you and Rufus can catch up with each other later,' she dismissed.

Annie was beginning to wish she had never set eyes on the man!

There was no doubting that Celia Diamond could be slightly condescending in her manner, or that things had become a little complicated since Anthony had arrived with his fiancée for a visit, but for the main part Annie had enjoyed her time here, found Jessica a delight to work with. Admittedly, it hadn't all been peace and harmony, but she loved Jessica, and anything else was just discomfort she had learnt to live with.

With the arrival of Rufus Diamond, she had a feeling all that was about to change!

CHAPTER TWO

'ISN'T it wonderful?' Jessica's eyes glowed deeply blue. 'Daddy's home!' She clapped her hands together in pleasure.

Annie wished she could share the young girl's enthusiasm, but, having made her escape from the man downstairs only minutes ago, she was in no hurry to see Rufus Diamond again. Although it was obvious, from Jessica's excitement, that his daughter couldn't wait for him to come back up to her bedroom.

'It's a lovely surprise for you,' Annie acknowledged guardedly, straightening the pillows behind her charge. 'Does your father often return unexpectedly in this way?'

'Always!' Jessica nodded happily, dark curls bouncing. 'But he leaves just as suddenly too,' she added wistfully.

Annie realised he probably had to; as an investigative reporter he would just have to go where the story was, whenever it occurred. Which was pretty tough on his young daughter. Although, she had to admit, Jessica seemed a well-adjusted child to her; she certainly didn't qualify as neglected or psychologically disturbed!

Annie herself was still puzzled as to what she could have said earlier to so amuse Rufus Diamond. Neither he nor Celia had offered an explanation before she'd excused herself to come upstairs to Jessica. And she had no intention of asking the little girl; that would be most unfair.

'How are you feeling this afternoon?' She smiled down at her young charge.

Jessica grinned back at her—her grin, Annie now knew, was not unlike her father's! 'Well enough to go downstairs for dinner!' she announced cheerfully.

Annie felt her heart sink at the statement. If Jessica went down to the family dining-room for the meal, then it meant she had to join them too. And if the tension between Celia and Rufus was any indication of the man's effect on the rest of the family it boded ill for everyone's digestion—including her own!

'Are you sure?' she prompted lightly. 'You're still using the crutches to get about.' The accident had happened at the weekend, three days ago, and Jessica had been advised by the doctor to rest for several days before attempting to put any stress on her ankle.

The first day or so Jessica had enjoyed being waited on, having visitors come up to her bedroom, but after that the novelty had begun to pall. Consequently, this morning she had announced she would get up for a while, although after a couple of hours' activity she had been happy to spend the afternoon back in her bed resting. But not now, with the arrival of her father, it seemed!

'Daddy will carry me down,' Jessica assured her warmly, obviously liking this idea very much.

'The sooner you get up on your own two feet, the sooner you can go back to school,' Annie teased the little girl.

Jessica's face lit up at the thought. 'Can I go back tomorrow?'

Annie laughed indulgently, knowing that the week Jessica had been told to take as sick-leave from the private day school she attended twenty miles away had been an added incentive to Jessica when it came to the bed-rest. But even that had started to fade as Jessica had begun to miss her schoolfriends, especially her best friend, Lucy.

'I think that may be a little soon.' Annie shook her head regretfully. 'Besides, you can spend some time with your father now.' Her humour faded at that thought; hopefully she wouldn't have to spend time with him too! 'Speaking of which,' she added briskly, 'I had better go and shower and dress for dinner so that I can come back and help you later.'

'Is Daddy coming back up soon?' Jessica frowned at his non-appearance.

Very soon, if the abruptness of his conversation with Celia was anything to go by! 'I'm sure he is.' Annie squeezed the little girl's hand reassuringly. 'He was just saying hello to your grandmother when I came up.'

Jessica grimaced at this news. 'Oh.'

Obviously the tension that existed between her father and Celia wasn't a family secret, not even from someone as young as Jessica!

'Try and get some rest,' Annie encouraged. 'Then you won't feel sleepy over dinner.'

She wished, as she walked slowly down the hallway to her own bedroom, that she could sleep through dinner; it didn't promise, with Rufus Diamond's arrival, to be a very restful meal.

'Annie!'

She turned sharply at the sound of her name being called, colour warming her cheeks as she saw Anthony hurrying towards her, her heart giving its usual leap of excitement just at the sight of him, his blond good looks breathtaking to say the least. Annie had been bowled over by him the first time she'd looked at him.

'God, I'm sorry about earlier.' He spoke agitatedly as he reached her side, hair windswept, sky-blue eyes troubled as he looked down at her. 'Davina decided she just had to go into town, and I just had to drive her because the weather was so bad.' He mimicked a good impression of the slightly breathless way his fiancée spoke. 'I hope you didn't wait too long for me down on the jetty,' he said apologetically as he took one of her hands into his.

Annie was mesmerised once again by the deep blue of his eyes, her legs feeling suddenly weak, her hand trembling when it made contact with his.

How had Rufus Diamond guessed that she was waiting for his brother down on the jetty?

More important than that, how had he known she had become romantically entangled with his brother?

Because she had. Had been attracted to Anthony from the first moment she'd looked at him when he'd come to stay several weekends ago. Too late she had realised he was engaged to someone else. An engagement which was virtually impossible for him to get out of.

'Not very long,' she dismissed, though she had already waited almost an hour when Rufus Diamond had arrived. She sounded slightly breathless herself because of Anthony's close proximity.

'I'm really sorry.' Anthony squeezed her hand, smiling. 'I know that we need to talk, that there must be things you want to ask me.'

Annie felt that fluttering sensation in her chest again

as she thought of the possibility that some of their conversation might concern how he felt about her! She wondered if he would kiss her again, as he had on Sunday.

His mother and Davina had gone off that morning to visit neighbouring friends for a couple of hours, and Anthony had cried off because he had some notes to prepare for a case he was involved in when he got back to London the following week. He had told her later that he had also hoped for an opportunity to be alone with her…!

In one way it was lucky he had stayed behind on Sunday, because he'd been the one to help her after Jessica had come off her horse, driving them to the hospital so that Jessica could have her ankle X-rayed, carrying the little girl up to her bedroom once they'd returned, sitting with them both until Jessica had fallen asleep.

And that was when he had kissed her…!

Annie had been stunned. Elated. Ecstatic. Because the attraction she had felt towards him, for so many weeks, was returned.

And then she had felt devastated. Embarrassed. Because he was engaged to marry another woman.

Anthony had explained that he no longer loved Davina, but that it was almost impossible for him to tell her so at this time, since Davina's father was the senior partner in the law firm Anthony worked for.

Annie could sympathise with his dilemma, but she had no idea where that left her. 'It doesn't matter,' she excused him now abruptly, still uncomfortable with the fact that he was engaged to Davina. 'I—your brother is home,' she stated flatly, not sure that she would be able to see much more of Anthony anyway, still wondering if she would have a job after today.

It was as if she had given Anthony an electric shock. He stepped back abruptly, releasing her hand as he did so. 'Rufus is back?' he grated incredulously, blue eyes wide open now.

'He's downstairs with your mother.' Annie nodded, feeling totally miserable about the other man's return herself. In fact, the only one who seemed pleased to see him was Jessica! 'I'm surprised you didn't see him on your way up,' she added heavily. Or hear him, she added silently: Rufus Diamond hadn't exactly been quiet over his disapproval at Jessica having a replacement nanny.

Anthony still frowned. 'I came straight upstairs to look for you. Do you know how long he's staying?'

'He's only just arrived!' she responded ruefully.

'His last effort to be a father to Jess amounted to a full twenty-four hours, I believe,' Anthony scorned. 'Have you seen him? Spoken to him?' He looked at her searchingly. 'I can see by your expression that you have,' he said disgustedly. 'Throwing his weight about as usual, no doubt?'

She moistened dry lips. 'He didn't seem—too happy about Margaret's departure.'

Anthony raised dark blond brows. 'I wonder why? I mean, a nanny is just a nanny— Oh, not you, of course, my darling,' he quickly apologised as she looked taken aback. 'But Jess has had a succession of nannies; I'm just surprised Rufus could tell one from another!'

Well, he certainly seemed to know the difference this time! Although Annie was still stunned by Anthony's endearment; was she really his darling?

'Margaret was a blonde; Annie is a redhead,' drawled

a voice that was becoming all too recognisable. 'I think even I can tell the difference,' Rufus Diamond said sarcastically as he strode down the hallway.

Annie was once again struck by the lack of similarity between these two men: Rufus was at least a couple of inches taller than his brother as he stood beside the younger man, his hair long, dark and shaggy, while Anthony's was blond and kept expertly styled. Rufus was also the more powerfully built, and even the casual clothing they both wore was of a completely different style; the older man wore jeans, whereas Anthony's trousers were tailored. And, although both men were strikingly handsome, that was in a completely different way, too: Anthony's was a boyish handsomeness, while Rufus Diamond's face looked as if it had been hewn from the rocks along the seashore.

If Rufus had heard that remark about Jessica's nannies, had he also heard his brother call her his darling?

Cobalt-blue eyes were narrowed on the two of them in cool assessment before he turned to look at his brother. 'Davina seems to be wondering where you've got to,' he went on pointedly. 'I told her to look for the first pretty face and she was sure to find you there! And I was right,' he added softly, his speculative gaze encompassing Annie again as well now.

She felt the colour enter her cheeks, could feel its warmth. And it had nothing to do with being called pretty by this man. Why was Rufus so contemptuous of her? He didn't even know her! From the way he talked to her, and about her, she didn't think he was going to take the time to get to know her, either!

'I was merely asking Anthony if he knew whether or

not you were coming up to see Jessica again,' she told him tartly. 'She seemed to think you would be.'

'And she was right, because here I am,' he returned, amusement—at her expense!—darkening his eyes even more.

She met that look unblinkingly. 'I'm sure Jessica will be thrilled,' she said evenly.

To her surprise Rufus threw back his head and gave a shout of laughter, his expression warm now, that grin still curving his lips as he looked down at her. 'I was wondering if this unusual colour was real or from a bottle.' He reached out and lightly ruffled the deep red of her short, curling hair. 'Now I know it is red! I should watch yourself with this one, Anthony,' he told his brother. 'She may just turn round and bite!' And, with that last taunt left floating in the air between them, he strode off to Jessica's bedroom, quietly going inside. Jessica's squeals of delight were heard seconds later.

'What did he mean by that last remark?' Anthony asked sharply. 'Exactly what did the two of you talk about when you met earlier?'

Annie smoothed her mussed hair with irritated fingers. Really, Rufus Diamond treated her as if she were no older than Jessica! Although, from the implications he was making concerning herself and his brother, he didn't really believe that...!

'Annie!' Anthony snapped impatiently. 'I asked what you and Rufus talked about earlier,' he prompted at her puzzled look.

She thought back to that embarrassing conversation with him on the beach, when she had mistaken him for a trespasser—and knew she couldn't tell Anthony about that. She felt uncomfortable enough about the encounter already, without sharing it with anyone.

'Not a lot,' she responded vaguely. 'Although he did tell me to be careful on the beach; he said someone had once died there.' She looked up at Anthony, perplexed.

He pursed his lips thoughtfully. 'Did he, indeed?' he said slowly. 'Did he say who it was?'

'No.' She shrugged. 'We really weren't talking for that long.' Only long enough for Annie to make a complete fool of herself!

'Hmm.' Anthony was still attentive. 'It's interesting that he told you about that at all.'

Annie was intrigued now. 'Is it?'

'It isn't important,' Anthony dismissed carelessly. 'Although you do realise, with Rufus around, we're going to have to be even more careful about when and where the two of us meet?'

She had been debating this afternoon, as she'd stood on the jetty waiting for him—pointlessly, as it turned out—whether or not they should meet again. Oh, she was no less attracted to him, and she wanted to feel wanted by him, but he was engaged to another woman—no matter how much of a farce, on his part, the engagement now was.

This was the circle in which she had kept going round and round, and every time she'd come back to the fact that she was attracted to a man who was engaged to marry someone else. Even though the attraction seemed to be reciprocated, it was still wrong for her to feel this way about a man promised to another girl.

She drew in a controlling breath. 'Perhaps we shouldn't meet...'

'I was hoping you would say that!' Anthony gave her

a hug, smiling down at her when he released her. 'It won't be for long; as I've said, going by Rufus's last visit, this one may only be for a day or so. Then we can start to see each other without worrying about him.'

That hadn't been what she was about to say at all. Much as it pained her, the only conclusion she had come to concerning her relationship with Anthony—such as it was!—was that it would have to end. At least until Anthony had decided what he was going to do about his engagement. But Anthony seemed to have misunderstood her just now...

'You really are wonderful, Annie,' he told her huskily, blue eyes glowing. 'How could I have been so stupid as to think I could make a go of things with Davina?' He shook his head at his own lack of forethought. 'I'll sort things out, Annie, you'll see. In the meantime, I intend to stay as much out of Rufus's way as possible. I suggest you do the same.'

Easier said than done!

As Jessica had hoped, Daddy did come and carry her downstairs to dinner. Which meant he came up to Jessica's bedroom to collect her. And as Annie was there too, having helped the young girl to dress in her prettiest dress—red velvet edged with fine lace at the neck and cuffs—she encountered Rufus again not much more than an hour later.

As the Diamonds were a family that dressed for dinner, his black evening suit, snowy white shirt and black bow-tie came as nothing of a surprise to Annie. The fact that the formality of his clothing did little to disguise the leashed power within was also expected; Rufus Diamond was a man who exuded arrogant masculinity.

'Does our little mouse still have her roar this evening?' he teased. 'Or has Anthony managed to talk you down to a whimper?'

Jessica looked puzzled by his query. 'But we don't have any mice, Daddy.'

Annie didn't pretend not to know it was her he was referring to. Usually she was so calm and controlled—temper tantrums hadn't gone down too well at the children's homes! It was only this man who brought back echoes of the fiery side of her nature that over the years she had taken such care to quell.

As he did now! 'The younger Mr Diamond doesn't talk down to me at all,' she told him tartly.

The humour left Rufus's darkly mocking face as he frowned, giving him a slightly menacing appearance—and making Annie wonder if she was wise to talk back to him so sharply. He was her employer, after all...

'Don't backtrack, Annie,' he replied curtly—as if he was well able to read her inner uncertainty.

Maybe he could. She had never been any good at hiding her feelings. Another reason for ending this barely formed relationship with Anthony. It could only bring her grief, and possibly dismissal from working with the little girl she already adored. These sort of complications weren't something she had given any thought to when she had opted to work in a family environment!

'And I wasn't talking down to you, either,' Rufus continued firmly. 'Jessica did nothing but extol your virtues for the earlier part of this evening.' He ruffled his daughter's hair affectionately, receiving a pleased giggle in return. Rufus turned back to Annie with darkly piercing eyes. 'Children aren't easily deceived.'

That was true; she had easily been able to tell, when she was in care, which people were genuinely interested in her and who was just making a show of being kind. But she didn't see how anyone could be less than sincerely fond of a lovely child like Jessica.

'Daddy…' Jessica spoke carefully. 'What does "extol your virtues" mean?' She wrinkled her nose in confusion.

'It means, young lady—' Rufus easily swung his daughter up into his arms, grinning down at her '—that you think Annie is great!'

'But she is,' Jessica said without a shadow of doubt.

'I'm sure she is, poppet.' Rufus tickled his daughter as he carried her ceremoniously down the wide staircase.

Annie walked happily along behind them, pleased with the obvious closeness between father and daughter, despite Rufus's three-month absence. The two could have been together only yesterday, so naturally affectionate was their relationship.

'Mind you,' Rufus paused to whisper conspiratorially to Jessica, 'when I met Annie earlier, I didn't think she was much older than you!' This last, playful remark was accompanied by a glance back at a red-faced Annie. 'She looks—much older in that black dress,' he added lightly, blue gaze challenging.

'I helped her to choose it,' Jessica told him proudly.

And, in fact, she had. Having worked in a daytime kindergarten, where her evenings were her own, Annie hadn't had much call for the sort of formal clothes she would need for one of the Diamond dinners. After two evenings of coming down in serviceable skirts and blouses, of feeling exactly what she was—the hired help—she had decided to change that, taking Jessica into town with her shopping on their first available Saturday and buying three dresses that, when matched with differing accessories, could get her through an evening no matter what company happened to arrive. On the very evening she'd bought the dresses she had been presented with a bishop and a judge, so her purchases had been well worth the effort!

She had bought black, royal-blue and white dresses, and tonight, as Rufus Diamond had duly noted, she wore the black one, which while not accentuating her figure, didn't hide it either, the above-knee length revealing an expanse of shapely leg too. On a couple of other evenings she had worn a long floral scarf trailing from her throat, or a fitted jacket of powder-blue, but tonight she wore only a single silver broach fastened above her left breast; she hadn't wanted to wear anything this evening that would draw attention to her!

'And Annie is much older than me,' Jessica added in a scandalised voice. 'She's twenty-two. She told me she is.'

'Oh, that's much older!' Rufus agreed, only the twitch of his lips, as he turned briefly to Annie, telling of his repressed humour—again at her expense.

'Really, Daddy.' Jessica unwittingly sounded just like her grandmother at that moment. 'You can be so silly at times.' She gave an exasperated shake of her head—again, not unlike Celia would have done.

Annie doubted that the word 'silly' could be applied to Rufus—at any time. It certainly wasn't the impression he had given her since their first meeting this afternoon!

And while Annie, in her parentless state, might have little idea of what a family dinner should be like, she was sure that the following couple of hours spent at the Diamond dining table was not it!

It was the strangest meal Annie had ever been present

at—and she didn't mean food-wise; as usual Mrs Wilson, the cook, had provided an excellent meal; home-made pâté, followed by duck in a delicious orange sauce, with fresh fruit in port to finish. But for all the justice the Diamond family paid it, it might as well have been the beans on toast Annie had often enjoyed in the past as her own meal of the day!

The tension around the table was intolerable, felt by all, she was sure, except Jessica—a happy Jessica with her father seated at her side. And Rufus Diamond was the catalyst for everyone else's tension—although for all the notice he took of it he might have been as unaware of it as his daughter.

Or so Annie thought...

Jessica was seated between the two of them, and Rufus had to lean forward to speak to Annie. 'Enjoying yourself?' he asked, still with that repressed humour.

She had been wishing the meal over, at least her own and Jessica's part in it. The young girl usually retired to bed when the coffee and port stage was reached. Although that might be different tonight, as her father was here...

As for enjoying the meal...! Celia was at her most haughty, while Davina, a tall, elegant blonde, flirted shamelessly with Rufus at every opportunity, and Anthony—well, Anthony seemed lost in his own reverie, paying little attention to any of them. This Annie was relieved about; the last thing she wanted was to give Rufus any more ammunition to fire at herself and Anthony!

'Very much, thank you,' she returned primly.

He gave that wolfish grin at her politeness. 'Liar!' he rejoined quietly.

She met his gaze unflinchingly. 'I was referring to the food, of course.'

Once again she was taken aback when he threw back his head and gave a throaty laugh of pure enjoyment, those lines she had noticed earlier beside his eyes and mouth proving to be laughter lines—evidence that this man laughed a lot. And she didn't think it was always at other people; somehow she sensed that he had the ability to laugh at himself too. This man was an enigma, a chameleon, one moment distant and forbidding, the next full of humour. It could take a lifetime to know such a man—

Annie broke off her thoughts with a guilty glance in Anthony's direction, once again affected by his good looks, the way he smiled across at her conspiratorially, almost as if he had sensed her confusion—although not, thank goodness, the reason for it. She doubted he would smile at her in that way if he realised exactly what she had been thinking about his brother!

'Would you care to share the joke with us, Annie?' Celia Diamond's mildly arrogant voice broke in on her thoughts. 'I'm sure we could all do with some light amusement,' she added dryly—showing she was far from immune to the awkwardness of the evening.

But as she and the rest of the family, and the tension that existed between them with Rufus's presence, were the subject of that light amusement Annie somehow didn't think the other woman would be at all happy to share the joke!

Annie shot Rufus a look that clearly cried 'help'—although, even knowing Rufus's sense of humour as little as she did, she had a feeling he might just enjoy sitting back and watching her squirm!

'It was just a little anecdote about Jessica that Annie wished to share with me.' Thankfully, Rufus did come to her rescue. 'Speaking of which,' he added, with an affectionate wink at his daughter, 'I think it's time Jess went up to bed. No protests, young lady,' he added with gentle reproof as he sensed that was exactly what she was about to give him. 'You're going to need plenty of sleep if you're going to attempt to beat me at chess tomorrow.'

This was the first indication Annie had had that the child played chess; she seemed very young to have mastered such a complicated game. Nevertheless Annie had stood up to leave quickly enough herself at Rufus's first suggestion of it; this evening couldn't end quickly enough as far as she was concerned!

Although Rufus's next comment warned her that, for her at least, it was far from over...!

'Carry on and have coffee without me,' he told his family as he easily swung Jessica back up into his arms. 'Once we have Jessica settled for the night, I intend talking to Annie for a while.'

It wasn't the easy dismissal of her own coffee that bothered her, nor even Rufus's casual grouping of the two of them, but that innocuous-sounding mention of 'talking to Annie for a while'...

What did Rufus want to talk to her about? The fact that she was the new nanny to his daughter? Or something else...?

CHAPTER THREE

'THESE are excellent references.' Rufus put the two letters he had just read down on the desk in front of him, his eyes narrowed thoughtfully. 'They must have been sorry to lose you at the kindergarten.'

It was a statement, not a question, Annie knew that—because Brenda Thompson, the person in charge of the kindergarten, had clearly said so in her letter of reference.

They were in Rufus Diamond's study, a spacious room furnished with heavy mahogany furniture; it was next to the library, and Annie hadn't even known it was here, let alone entered it before. Not that this particularly surprised her: Clifftop House was an enormous place, with two completely self-contained wings at either end of it. One housed the servants who lived in, the other appeared to be unused, and there were dozens of rooms that Annie had never been into.

Rufus had kissed his daughter goodnight once they were upstairs, leaving Annie to prepare the little girl for bed and informing her that he would see her downstairs in his study as soon as she had finished what she was doing. Annie had had to ask Jessica for directions to her father's study.

As she sat across the desk from him now, it was as if those moments of humour between them earlier had never happened. She felt like one of the children at the home, hauled before Mrs James for some misdemeanour

37

or other! Not that she ever had been. Keep your head down and stay out of trouble—that had been her motto. It had seemed to work quite well—

'Excellent references,' Rufus repeated slowly, the removal of his jacket and loosening of his bow-tie not making him look any more approachable. 'But they actually tell me very little about you. Who are you? Where are your family? Are you likely to leave at a moment's notice too?' he added grimly, obviously thinking of the absent Margaret. 'I think I have a right to ask these questions; after all, you are in charge of my daughter on a day-to-day basis.'

Annie agreed with him, knew she would be the same if her own daughter's welfare were at stake. And yet, from Rufus Diamond, these questions seemed an intrusion. It was totally illogical, but she found she didn't want to tell him any more about herself than she had to.

'I'm Annie Fletcher. And I'm your typical Orphan Annie,' she added self-derisively. 'I have no family that I'm aware of. And I wouldn't leave here, or Jessica, without giving you a good reason—and time enough to find a replacement!'

His mouth twisted. 'I believe Margaret told me the same thing.'

She shrugged. 'You'll have to take that up with Margaret; I never met her.' Jessica had been without a nanny for almost a week when Annie had arrived two months ago. 'All I can say is that I won't do the same thing.'

'Take it or leave it, hmm?' Rufus said shrewdly.

'I didn't mean that at all,' Annie defended quietly, hot colour in her cheeks. 'Of course you don't have to take it or leave it; you're my employer, and you're perfectly within your rights to want certain assurances. I seriously doubt I would ever choose to leave Jessica.' Her expression softened as she spoke of the child.

Dark eyes assessed her questioningly. 'You're fond of my daughter?'

'Very.' She didn't take offence at the question—not this one—although she felt sure there were plenty of others Rufus Diamond could and would ask that would be very offensive indeed!

'And just how fond of my brother are you?'

That was one of them! It wasn't altogether unexpected, though; she had known since the three of them met in the hallway earlier that Rufus would have to make some reference to it. She wasn't disappointed!

'I like all the family,' she said evasively.

Rufus's mouth thinned. 'Even Celia?' he queried.

The other woman could be extremely haughty, and Annie knew now she considered her a servant. But at least Celia was honest about it, made no pretence of it being otherwise, and for the main part she had treated Annie fairly, if not exactly warmly.

'Even Celia,' she confirmed firmly.

Rufus gave a humourless grin. 'Methinks the lady doth protest too much,' he said smoothly.

'Not at all,' Annie protested indignantly. 'Mrs Diamond has been very kind in her own way.' She regretted adding the last comment almost as soon as she had said it, knowing she had given Rufus an opening she hadn't meant to. She didn't have to wait long!

'"In her own way",' Rufus retorted. 'I've known Celia since I was two years old—and I've never seen her be kind to anyone. Not without a damn good reason!'

He added cynically, 'And nannies to my daughter do not come under that category.'

Annie wasn't particularly interested in his scathing comments concerning Celia, had no intention of getting into any sort of in-depth conversation concerning the other woman. What did interest her was Rufus's reference to knowing Celia since he was two years old... Of course, most children didn't begin to learn things about their parents until they were a few years old, but in this case she didn't think that was what was meant...

Rufus was watching her closely, well aware of her puzzlement, she was sure. The man seemed to miss nothing!

'You really don't know too much about this family, do you?' he said slowly.

She knew she loved Jessica, that Celia lived her role as lady of the manor to perfection—and that Anthony was trapped in an engagement he shouldn't be in! What else did she need to know?

'Perhaps I should get back to my original question.' Rufus spoke purposefully now, dark eyes watchful. 'How well do you know Anthony?'

Not well enough, obviously. Because until this last weekend she hadn't even realised he had a fiancée. He had been down for several weekend visits on his own, which was when Annie had found herself becoming attracted to his charm and good looks. It had been a shock—and a disappointment—when he had arrived on Saturday with Davina, to stay for a week. Then he had kissed her on Sunday... Now she was just confused about the whole thing.

'I don't,' she answered honestly. Did you have to know a person well to be attracted to them?

Rufus was still watching her with those shrewdly assessing eyes. 'In that case,' he finally said harshly, 'my advice to you is stay well away from him!'

She remained outwardly calm, but flinched inwardly at the force behind Rufus's words. It had been obvious from the first that there was little love lost between the two brothers, and that the dislike was mutual. But once more Rufus Diamond was talking to her as if she were no older than Jessica. Maybe falling for the charm of a man who had turned out to be engaged to marry another woman wasn't the most sensible thing she had ever done in her life, but, as Jessica had pointed out earlier, she was much older than her young charge—old enough to make her own mistakes, or otherwise!

'Fatherly advice, Mr Diamond?' she returned smartly.

His mouth tightened as her barb hit home. 'I was only joking with Jessica earlier when I made that remark about your age.' He easily guessed which comment of his she had taken exception to. 'I also take back what I said down on the beach, about your being young and impressionable,' he added at her bemused expression. 'Young you may be, but you're nobody's fool.'

Annie drew in a sharp breath; she wasn't so sure about that!

The fact remained that she hadn't known about Anthony's fiancée until Saturday, but even when she had found out she had still allowed him to kiss her. Wasn't that foolish in the extreme, even if she did feel so deeply attracted to him?

'Thank you,' she accepted huskily, not quite able to meet the deep blue of Rufus's gaze.

'And whether my advice just now was fatherly or not,' he continued briskly, 'you would do well to take it!'

She bristled indignantly. Rufus had arrived here only a few short hours ago, and yet he seemed to have done nothing in that time but issue orders and upset people—mostly her! And, while she accepted he had a right to tell her what he required of her as far as Jessica was concerned, she did not welcome his interference in what she considered to be her private life!

Nevertheless, she chose her next words carefully. 'You're very kind, Mr Diamond—'

'I'm no more kind than Celia,' he cut in scathingly. 'Anthony either, for that matter. In fact, we aren't a very kind family,' he concluded.

'In that case, I'm surprised you leave—' She broke off abruptly, warned by the sudden dark anger in his face that she would be overstepping the line with the observation she was about to make concerning Jessica. She looked up at him with wide, apprehensive eyes as he stood up forcefully, his size seeming to fill the room.

'Not young and impressionable at all,' he said with deliberation. 'And for God's sake take that scared-rabbit look off your face,' he told her disgustedly, moving around the desk to perch on it in front of her. 'I may not be kind, Annie, but by the same token I've never struck a woman in my life. And I don't intend to start with you. Even if you do say the damnedest things,' he added gratingly. 'I leave Jessica here because there is nowhere else for her to go. Her mother is dead.' It was a flat statement of fact, revealing none of his inner feelings concerning the loss. 'And I can hardly take her with me when I go on an assignment!'

Annie could see the sense of that; she also knew that Jessica fared so much better than she had herself. Her own mother had died shortly after giving birth to her, and she had never even known who her father was, only the circumstances of her birth. Whereas Jessica obviously adored her father, for all his long absences.

Annie moistened her lips. 'I'm sorry; I didn't mean to criticise—'

'Yes, you did,' he said without rancour. 'And I probably deserve it.' He reached out to put his hand beneath her chin and gently raise her face so that she had no choice but to look directly into his. He didn't look angry any more, his mouth curving into a smile. 'You'll do, Annie Fletcher,' he told her huskily. 'You love my daughter; that's all the reference you need.' He easily dismissed the two letters she had provided.

She was barely breathing, certainly not moving, very conscious of how very close they were, the deep cobalt-blue of his eyes so clear to her now—the only thing that was—as her gaze was held mesmerised by his, her face made immobile by the touch of his hand, his fingers warm against the softness of her throat.

She flicked her tongue over her lips again, colour warming her cheeks as she saw his eyes following the movement. She inwardly withdrew, then instantly moved back from the touch of his hand, gratefully drawing air into her lungs at the same time. What on earth was happening to her? She *wasn't* that young and impressionable—so how, feeling the way she did about Anthony, had she also felt the pull of this man's attraction?

She didn't know herself under these circumstances. But she was sure that, even if the Diamond men weren't kind, they were both possessed of an attractiveness she would be better off without!

'Can I go now?' she said abruptly, wishing he would move away from her—let her breathe a little!

Thankfully, he did, moving back behind the desk, although he didn't sit down again, merely looked at her from beneath lowered lids. 'No,' he finally replied forcefully. 'We haven't talked about Jessica's accident yet.'

Which was one of the things she was here to discuss; how could she have forgotten? This man, that was how; she was finding it difficult to keep up with his lightning changes of mood and conversation, knew she would look back on this time spent in his study with a feeling of exhaustion. She felt as if she had to constantly be on her guard, for one reason or another.

And the subject of Jessica's accident was no different. She didn't know how it had happened; one minute the little girl had been in the saddle, the next she had been on the ground. Annie was a novice rider herself; simply managing to stay seated in the saddle was a major feat! She had mastered just sitting on the back of the placid animal she had been given and letting the horse do all the work. She simply wasn't experienced enough to give any sort of judgement on Jessica's mishap.

That in itself would probably be a black mark against her in Rufus Diamond's book!

'Knowing how to ride a horse wasn't something that was discussed when I came here for an interview,' she told him defensively. 'But it's something Jessica loves to do, and as she can't possibly go out on her own—'

'You had to accompany her,' Rufus surmised, his eyes suddenly alight with humour, a slight twitch to those sculptured lips. 'Done much riding before, have you, Annie?' He raised innocently questioning brows.

Too innocently. He was laughing at her again, damn him!

'There wasn't much call for it in the inner London Children's home I was brought up in!' she told him sharply.

The stark contrast between her own childhood and Jessica's was apparent in that one blunt statement. There had never been too much spare cash at the home, certainly not enough to run to riding lessons. Even if she had wanted them. Which she hadn't.

And after Jessica's accident she wasn't sure she ever wanted to sit on a horse again! Jessica had been riding most of her life, it seemed, and still she had been thrown.

'So you meant it literally when you called yourself Orphan Annie?' Rufus said.

'Yes.' She was on the defensive, unsure of the turn of the conversation. Again!

Rufus took his time, sitting down in the chair behind the desk, his face softening as he looked across its width at her. 'In that case, I wouldn't take the Diamond family as a typical example of the species,' he drawled dryly. 'It had some sense of normality before my father died six years ago; since then it's deteriorated into anarchy,' he said matter-of-factly. 'A group of people who happen to share the same house but who can barely stand the sight of each other!'

'Surely not?' Annie gasped in dismay at the tragedy of such a thing. But hadn't she seen it herself this evening, in the barely maintained civility over dinner? And at the time she had thought Rufus to be the catalyst; she couldn't remember it having been quite as tense on other evenings when she and Jessica had joined in the evening meal.

'Surely, yes,' Rufus confirmed wryly. 'And as no one else seems to have filled you in on the family history perhaps I should do so,' he said wearily.

She wasn't sure she wanted to know, already felt uncomfortable enough with the little she did know. 'Is it relevant to Jessica that I know?' She frowned.

His mouth tightened. 'Before the weekend, I would have said no. Now I'm not so sure...' He grimaced darkly, then shook off that mood as he smiled across at her. 'Don't look so worried,' he chided, at her apprehensive expression. 'As far as I'm aware, there is no history of axe murderers or serial killers in the family. At least, none that Celia would ever allow to be discussed! Appearances are everything to my dear stepmama,' he told her wryly. 'Although she wasn't always so particular,' he amended harshly, eyes cold with anger once again.

'Stepmama'... Celia was his stepmother.

His earlier comments made complete sense now. Although it meant a bit of readjusting in Annie's own mind, she freely admitted. He and Anthony were half-brothers, which explained the stark contrast in their colouring, the fact that the two men shared so few characteristics. Oh, they were both handsome men, but in a completely different way. It also explained the lack of genuine affection between Rufus and Celia. Although Rufus could surely only have been a baby when Celia married his father...

Rufus was watching her with amusement. 'Your arithmetic is perfectly in order. I was barely two when my own mother died. And Celia, my father's secretary at the time, stepped in to help him over his loss. She did such a good job of it that Anthony was born exactly six months after their hurriedly arranged wedding!' he scorned. 'I'm not judging their morals, Annie,' he explained as she frowned a little more. 'Merely the lack of mourning accorded my own mother.'

She wasn't frowning because she thought he was being judgemental where his father and Celia's morals were concerned; it didn't seem to matter nowadays when so many children were born into relationships that didn't have a piece of paper to legalise them. No, she had been frowning at the speed of his father's second marriage after his wife's death, not the reason for it.

'That doesn't mean your father didn't mourn,' she told Rufus gently. 'Sometimes, when you've loved someone very much, to lose them is to lose part of yourself, and to love someone new is the only way you can feel complete again.'

Rufus looked at her closely, shaking his head slightly, as if he was surprised at her astuteness. 'You're very wise for someone so young, Annie—and again, I wasn't talking down to you,' he added quickly. 'My father said something along the same lines when I was old enough to question him on the subject. Unfortunately,' he continued hardily, 'by this time he had realised what a terrible mistake he had made in choosing Celia as his second love!'

It was often the case in rebound love, but in this instance they had produced a child. And the marriage had survived. Although, judging by Rufus's bitterness on his father's behalf towards Celia, not exactly happily.

So Rufus had grown up with a stepmother he disliked, and a half-brother he despised...

For years Annie had wished her own mother hadn't died when she was only a baby, had longed for a family of her own. But if the Diamond family were any example…!

'I did warn you not to take us as a typical family,' Rufus reminded her as he once more seemed to read her thoughts. 'Still want to work with Jessica?'

'Most definitely,' she answered without hesitation. 'And I'm really sorry about her accident. One moment she was in the saddle, the next the two of them were on the ground and Jessica was crying.' She could still remember that awful moment when she'd realised Jessica had really hurt herself.

'The two of them?' He looked puzzled.

'Jessica and the saddle.' She nodded. 'Didn't she tell you it came off with her?'

'No,' he rasped. 'Who the hell saddled the horse for her?'

'James, I presume…' Annie answered slowly, knowing by the darkening of Rufus's expression that the knowledge boded ill for the man in charge of the Diamond stables, which were situated at the back of the large house.

Jessica was very fond of the taciturn old man, and always managed to bring a smile to his weather-lined face—which probably accounted for why Jessica hadn't told her father about the saddle coming off with her when she fell… Oh, dear!

'The strap that goes under the horse came undone. I'm sure there was nothing James could have done about it.' She tried to make amends for her earlier gaffe.

Rufus drew in a deeply controlling breath, his jaw clenched. 'Probably not,' he muttered tightly.

But it was a subject he intended to pursue, the grimness of his expression told her.

Annie looked around for some way of diverting his attention, her sight resting with some relief on the chess-set that stood on a table in the corner of the wood-panelled room. 'I had no idea Jessica could play chess.' She referred to the challenge Rufus had issued to his daughter earlier for a match tomorrow. 'She seems very young to have mastered such a complicated game.'

'She asked me to teach her when she was five.' This was obviously an achievement of his young daughter's that he was proud of. 'She's quite good too,' he added ruefully. 'Although she hasn't managed to beat me yet!'

Annie doubted that many people had bested this man at anything. 'Yet,' she echoed mischievously. 'I know exactly how determined Jessica can be.'

He chuckled softly. 'A trait she inherited from her father, do you think?'

Now it was Annie's turn to give him an innocent look. 'I wouldn't know,' she returned mildly, eyes glowing with fun, a slight curve to her lips as she held back her smile.

His laughter deepened. 'I'll just bet you wouldn't! You—' He looked up sharply as the study door opened behind Annie without warning. 'What the hell do you want?' Rufus barked over Annie's shoulder at the in-truder. 'And isn't it usual to knock before entering a room?' he demanded of his brother.

Anthony was completely undaunted, Annie could see, now that she had half turned in her seat to look at the doorway. And as he looked at her accusingly she began to feel guilty about the laughter he must have heard be-tween Rufus and herself as he'd approached the study. Then she rebuked herself for feeling guilty; Rufus was her employer, Anthony was the one engaged to another woman!

'I was passing Jessica's room just now,' Anthony informed them disapprovingly, 'and she said her ankle was too painful for her to sleep. I gave her one of the pills the doctor left for her, but I have a feeling she really just wanted you to go up and see her again.'

Annie had stood up to go to her charge the moment Anthony had said she was in pain, but she hesitated at his last remark, looked uncertainly at Rufus.

He stood up. 'I'll go up to her,' he said decisively. 'It seems our conversation is over anyway.' He shot Anthony an impatient glance.

A gesture Anthony was completely impervious to. He grinned unconcernedly, his bad humour of moments ago seeming to have evaporated. 'Can I help it if your daughter loves you?' He shrugged, obviously having only recently left the dinner table, his hair looking blonder than ever against the dark material of the dinner jacket he still wore.

Rufus strode purposefully across the room, passing close to his brother as he did so, the differences between them at once noticeable, and it wasn't only in their colouring. Anthony's body kept trim and muscular from regular trips to the gym, whereas Rufus's lifestyle seemed to keep him slim and powerful, his slightly scornful expression seeming to say he didn't have time for such niceties as a gym, that the mere battle of life had hardened him physically as well as emotionally.

'It's as well someone does,' he muttered now in reply to Anthony's baiting comment, turning briefly back to Annie before going through the doorway he now stood before. 'Tell me, Annie,' he said. 'Do you play chess?'

She was taken aback at his return to the conversation Anthony had interrupted. But then, most of their discussion had been fragmented! 'Yes,' she answered huskily, not altogether sure why he was asking.

'I thought you might.' He nodded his satisfaction with her answer. 'We'll have a game together one evening. Although I should warn you, I never deliberately let anyone else win!'

She had a feeling that was true of him in most aspects of his life; he was a man who would give no quarter, to himself or anyone else! 'I never for a moment believed you would,' she acknowledged ruefully.

'Good.' He stepped out into the hallway, before once again pausing, turning back to her. 'Oh, and Annie…?'

What now? 'Yes?'

'You do look lovely in that black dress,' he told her throatily, a glitter of triumph in his eyes as he saw the blush on her cheeks before he turned and walked away, a quiet whistle floating in the air behind him.

Annie stared after him in dismay, knowing he had made that last comment to cause mischief; Jessica hadn't said she looked lovely earlier, only older! But she knew, as Anthony's mouth tightened in irritation, that Rufus's jibe had hit the target it was meant for.

She shook her head disbelievingly; these two men were like two little boys trying to score points off each other. For men aged thirty-nine and thirty-six, it was incredibly destructive…!

Anthony looked at her scowlingly. 'You and Rufus seem to be getting on well together.' It was more of an accusation than an observation!

'He seems happy enough that I continue to work with Jessica.' She deliberately didn't rise to the bait, having no intention of becoming yet another bone of contention between these two: they already shared enough ill feeling, without adding her to it! Besides, Rufus had meant to cause mischief…

Anthony cheered up at the statement. 'Well, that's good, isn't it? For us, I mean,' he said happily, moving closer to her. 'It means we'll have more time to get to know each other.'

Annie looked up at him, once again dazzled by his charming good looks, his normally pleasant disposition having returned. 'I suppose so,' she said slowly.

Anthony's arms moved smoothly about the smallness of her waist as he pulled her close against him.

'Someone might see us,' she protested.

'Who cares?' he dismissed. 'Besides, my mother and Davina are deep in discussion about some boring subject or other. I'd much rather be here with you.'

But Davina was his fiancée. This couldn't be right; Annie knew it couldn't. She tried to move gently but firmly out of his arms. 'Anthony—'

'Oh, for goodness' sake!' He thrust her away from him as he felt her struggle against him, a flush to his cheeks as he looked down at her. 'You weren't so damned particular on Sunday when I kissed you.' His eyes narrowed suspiciously. 'Or is it that, having met my older brother, you think he might be a better prospect?'

She gasped at the injustice of that accusation. She hadn't meant for that kiss to happen between them, had been racked with guilt about it ever since, very conscious of his engagement, no matter how disastrous that might appear to be. She certainly had no romantic interest in Rufus Diamond…! That would be pure madness on her part, even more so than her attraction to Anthony.

'I'm sorry, Annie.' Anthony was instantly contrite as he saw the tears sparkling in her eyes, once again holding her close to him. 'I shouldn't take my jealousy out on you.' He shook his head in self-disgust. 'Do you forgive me?' he encouraged softly, his forehead resting lightly on hers as he easily held her gaze.

How could she resist him when he looked exactly like a little boy, no older than some of the children she had looked after?

'Of course I forgive you,' she told him huskily. 'But Rufus is my employer, nothing else.' She pushed firmly from her mind her complete awareness of the older man.

'I'm glad you said that.' Anthony nodded his satisfaction. 'Because I would hate for Rufus to hurt you simply because he has an old score to settle with me.'

Annie looked up at him, troubled. Surely he wasn't referring to his mother's marriage to Rufus's father, and his own birth soon afterwards? No matter what Rufus considered to be the sins of the mother, they wouldn't have been passed on to an innocent child...

'I met Joanna first, you see,' he sighed, grimacing as Annie looked even more confused. 'Rufus's wife,' he explained wistfully. 'We met in London when I was at university there, had something of a—relationship,' he admitted. 'But it all ended when I came back here. At least, as far as I was concerned it did.' He shrugged. 'Unfortunately, Joanna hadn't taken our affair as lightly as I had, and she followed me down here, got a job locally, and once I had convinced her I didn't want our relationship to continue she set her sights on Rufus. Initially, I'm sure, to pique my interest. Which it didn't.' He grimaced again. 'But that just seemed to make Joanna more determined where Rufus was concerned, and before I knew what was happening the two of them were married. As Joanna related to me afterwards, her wedding gift to Rufus was to tell him I had been her lover first!'

Annie gasped at the cruelty of such a thing, no longer surprised at the animosity between the two men. Rufus was a man who would hate knowing his brother had been his wife's lover before their marriage!

'I hadn't mentioned my relationship with Joanna to Rufus because I really didn't think he was serious about her.' Anthony shook his head. 'I don't think he's ever really forgiven me for that.'

But the marriage had survived, and the couple had had Jessica together. Otherwise Annie wouldn't be here at all.

She had wanted to work with a family, had deliberately chosen to do so—but what a complicated family the Diamonds were turning out to be—the first Diamond bride dead, Celia becoming the wicked stepmother, Rufus's own bride tainted in a way he would never have been happy with, and she a Diamond bride who had also died.

Could it possibly have been one of these two women who had committed suicide in that rocky cove below Clifftop House? And, if so, which one...?

CHAPTER FOUR

'I TAKE it your interview last night with my stepson went well?' Celia Diamond queried briskly as she sat forward to pour the coffee that had just been brought in to them in Celia's private sitting-room.

Annie had answered the summons to join the other woman for morning coffee with some trepidation. But Jessica was in her father's study playing the promised game of chess, so she didn't really have a valid excuse not to join Celia.

She chose her words carefully, not really sure in her own mind of the success, or otherwise, of that meeting with Rufus. 'He seemed satisfied with my references,' she replied noncommittally.

Celia narrowed pale blue eyes. 'So you're to stay?'

Annie drew in a deep breath. 'It would seem so,' she said slowly.

'Good.' Celia sighed her satisfaction with this reply, then started sipping her coffee thoughtfully. 'I doubt that Rufus will stay here very long, anyway,' she said after a while. 'He never does!'

Well, Annie sincerely hoped that this time, for Jessica's sake he would. Although she could understand why he didn't usually prolong his visits—the tension in the house, since his arrival yesterday, was so tangible you could almost reach out and touch it!

'And I'm so glad you're to stay,' Celia continued evenly. 'Davina and I were discussing the wedding last night after we all had dinner, and it will be much easier for everyone involved if we don't have the added worry of Jessica's care to think of.'

'Wedding?' Annie echoed numbly. She could think of only one wedding Davina would want to discuss—her own! Was this the 'boring subject' the two women had discussed, that Anthony had referred to when he'd sought Annie out last night? She had a feeling that it was...

'The wedding has been brought forward to Christmas,' Celia explained, seemingly unaware of Annie's distress. 'Which, as it's to take place in London, means a lot of rearranging. The reception will be the problem, of course, because on such short notice we could end up with somewhere ghastly, and— But I'm sure all of this can't be of any interest to you,' she dismissed lightly. 'I merely want to assure myself that you will be here to take care of Jessica.'

Did she? Was that really all Celia wanted to do? Annie wasn't so sure. Or was it simply that she was looking for hidden meanings in everything now? Until yesterday she had taken all the Diamond family at face value; today she seemed to be looking for double meanings in every statement. It was Rufus's doing, of course. There was no way Celia could possibly know of her attraction to Anthony, and his interest in her. Was there...?

She was doing it again! Stop this, she inwardly berated herself, picking up her own cup of coffee and sipping it, grateful for the distraction. Poor Anthony; it seemed he was being pushed into this marriage from all sides!

Her coffee drunk, the conversation concluded to her

satisfaction—whatever that might be!—Celia excused herself, saying that she had some flowers to arrange and they were having guests to dinner this evening.

It was just Annie's luck that as she left the sitting-room immediately after Celia Anthony should be descending the stairs. They had parted in Rufus's study the previous evening, Anthony giving her a brief kiss on the lips before he went back to join his mother and Davina. A mother and a fiancée who had been discussing his forthcoming marriage. To say Annie was confused was putting it mildly!

Anthony gave her a searching look. 'Anything wrong?'

Yes, he was going to be married at Christmas, a matter of months away! And last night he had kissed her—again. Of course there was something wrong! But she was as much at a loss over what to do about it as she had been yesterday, down on the jetty.

'Anthony, I think we need to talk,' she began. 'Your mother has just told me—'

'About the wedding!' His grimaced his own feelings about that subject. 'Don't worry, Annie, it won't happen.'

She looked up at him with dark brown eyes, lashes long and silky. Because of her? She wasn't sure she wanted that responsibility, her own feelings towards him in total confusion. Since Rufus's arrival…

'And when do you intend telling Davina that?' she challenged. 'When the two of you reach the altar?'

Anthony's mouth tightened at the undoubted rebuke. 'I think that's my business, don't you?' he snapped resentfully.

Not because of her, she realised thankfully, noticing

things about him today that hadn't been visible when she'd been blinded by his charm and obvious good looks. With his anger came a slight twist of cruelty to his mouth, a coldness to his eyes, and—

'Hey, stop looking so worried,' he cajoled smilingly, that cruelty and coldness instantly gone, the laughter back in his eyes. 'I'm not really angry with you.' He grasped her arms lightly. 'Just a bit frustrated with the situation. Come on, Annie,' he encouraged softly. 'Smile for me.'

She was still confused, and it wasn't a situation she was comfortable with at all. 'I—'

'Trouble in paradise?' mocked a voice that was becoming increasingly familiar, Annie turning with a start to see Rufus coming down the hallway towards them, a sardonic grin curving those sculptured lips.

He looked taller than ever today, almost predatory in a black silk shirt and black denims, his dark hair long and unruly, even his eyes appearing black.

Annie had seen him only briefly earlier when he'd come to collect Jessica for her game of chess, and she found she was looking at him differently with the knowledge of what his marriage to Joanne must have been like. His arrogance was unmistakably an integral part of his nature, and she could only wonder at the blow his pride must have taken when he'd realised Anthony had been Joanne's lover—first...!

His eyes rested on her as he reached the two of them, one brow raised in silent query. It was a question Annie would never answer, wishing she didn't have knowledge of his wife at all, that Anthony had never told her. It gave Rufus a vulnerability she would never have associated with him otherwise.

Rufus's gaze hardened as he turned to his brother. 'You were born a century out of time, Anthony,' he rasped contemptuously. 'This fascination you have with the female members of the household staff—no offence intended, Annie,' he added mock-apologetically before turning back to Anthony with cold black eyes. 'It would have been more understandable a hundred years ago—although no more acceptable!'

Anthony had released Annie the moment his brother had first spoken, a flush to his cheeks now. 'At least I can appreciate a beautiful woman when I see one!' He returned the insult.

Rufus remained unmoved by the open retaliation in his brother's voice. 'You're engaged to a beautiful woman,' he replied. 'I suggest that in future you stick to her.' He took a firm grip of Annie's arm. 'And leave innocents like Annie alone!'

She felt like a bone argued over by two equally determined dogs! Besides, she didn't like the way Rufus, when it suited him, treated her as being no older than Jessica...

'That's rather a big assumption to have made on my behalf on so short an acquaintance,' she told him pleasantly as she quietly but firmly moved out of his grasp, meeting his gaze squarely.

'Are you saying you aren't an innocent?'

They might have been the only two people standing there, their eyes locked in silent battle.

She wasn't a complete innocent, had had her share of boyfriends in the past, but in the true sense of the word, in the way that Rufus meant—

'Anthony, darling.' Davina Adams strolled down the stairs behind them, a tall, willowy blonde of twenty-eight, and beautiful, as Rufus had already stated. 'My headache is better now.' She smiled at her fiancé, her wide blue eyes seeming to take in the tension surrounding the three at the bottom of the stairway—then dismissing it. 'Shall we go for that drive into town now? We could have some lunch out too,' she continued lightly. 'Rufus. Annie.' She acknowledged them rather belatedly before turning back questioningly to her fiancé.

Annie had met Davina for the first time over the weekend, and she was no nearer getting past that outer façade of charm to the real person beneath than she had been then. Perhaps it wasn't a veneer. But if that was the case, then Davina was a very shallow person, seeming to have no other interests than shopping, and her own appearance. But, nevertheless, she was very beautiful...

'Fine,' Anthony agreed easily. 'If you'll excuse us?' he threw carelessly at Annie and Rufus, Davina clinging to his arm as the two of them left the house.

'When Davina says jump, he jumps,' Rufus drawled into the silence that followed their departure.

Annie looked up at him frowningly. Exactly what did he mean by that remark?

'But she is very beautiful,' Rufus added.

'Yes,' Annie agreed flatly.

'And rich.'

'Yes...'

'It's a fact of life, Annie—' Rufus shrugged '—that my brother has already gone through most of his inheritance, and that he does have expensive tastes. And there's no getting away from the fact that Davina is a very wealthy young woman.'

Annie frowned. 'And I'm obviously not?'

Rufus frowned too now. 'I don't believe we were discussing you, Annie,' he said curtly. 'Were we…?'

This man was an investigative reporter, and it had never been more obvious to her than at this moment how good he was at his job. She had just given him information he hadn't asked for, had confirmed, without actually saying the words, her own interest in Anthony! Albeit an interest she was no longer sure of…

'No,' she responded briskly. 'Shall I go to Jessica now?' She deliberately resumed her role as his employee. 'I'm sure you must have things to do.'

'I do.' He nodded, still looking at her intently. 'Apparently I'm taking you out for lunch. The two of you. At Jessica's request,' he added—as if he sensed the refusal she had been about to make.

Her refusal had been purely instinctive, a wish not to spend any more time in Rufus Diamond's company than she needed to. But his mention of Jessica reminded her of exactly what she was doing here!

'Of course,' she accepted coolly. 'I'll just go up and get Jessica's coat.' She turned to ascend the stairs.

'Annie…?'

She had almost reached the top of the wide staircase—almost escaped what now felt like an emotional battering. Rufus Diamond was not a relaxing man to be around; in fact, he was the opposite. She felt as if she constantly had to be on her guard around him.

She drew in a deep breath, turning slowly. He stood exactly where she had left him, tall and infinitely powerful, despite the obvious grandeur of the surrounding reception area and wide curved staircase. Master of all he surveyed!

'Yes?' Even to her own ears her voice sounded apprehensive!

He grinned at her, that slightly wolfish grin that was so disarmingly charming. 'I'll beard the lioness in her den and tell Celia we're all deserting her for lunch!'

Her breath left her in a relieved sigh at the innocuousness of his comment—the first indication she had had that she was still holding it in! 'Fine.' She nodded dismissively.

'Oh, and Annie...?'

She had reached the top of the stairs now, had thought he had finished with her, turning impatiently as she realised he hadn't. Was he doing this on purpose? The laughter in those deep blue eyes seemed to say he was!

'Yes, Rufus?' she replied ruefully.

The grin widened, those laughter lines appearing now beside his nose and mouth. 'Don't bother to change on my account; you look good in denims too!'

The appreciative look he gave her told her he had been watching her as she'd walked up the stairs, and she was suddenly very conscious of the fit of her jeans as they clung to the curve of her bottom and long, slender legs.

'I wasn't about to,' she told him waspishly, finally making good her escape, but she could hear his laughter following her as she hurried down the hallway to collect coats for Jessica and herself, hot colour in her cheeks as she realised she was the reason for his amusement.

And she now had to spend the next few hours in the man's company! Wonderful! She was already starting to regret her earlier wish that Rufus would stay longer this time; now she hoped he would soon leave again!

Although later she felt really guilty for wanting that

as she watched Jessica's pleasure in having her father's company for a few hours. Jessica obviously adored him, and the affection was more than reciprocated. Whatever might have gone wrong in his marriage, Rufus Diamond loved his daughter very much.

Annie stood slightly outside of the relationship, feeling slightly superfluous as Jessica turned to her father for all her needs.

'You look sad all of a sudden.' Rufus softly interrupted her reverie, another indication Annie had that he had been watching her without her being aware of it. 'Nothing I've said or done, I hope?' He quirked that left brow of his in the disconcerting way he had, looking at her closely.

They had gone for a drive before stopping off at a pub for a light lunch, where Jessica was in her element seated between the two adults, her good humour unmistakable. And Annie had realised, in the last few minutes, that if Rufus ever decided to return home permanently she would no longer be needed. At the same time she knew how selfish her thoughts were, that it would be much better for Jessica to have her father at home with her than to be in the care of a hired nanny.

'No,' she assured him wistfully. He hadn't said or done anything; he just was who he was, and Jessica adored him.

Rufus still looked concernedly at her over the top of his daughter's head. 'Sure?'

'Sure.' She gave him a bright, meaningless smile. He wasn't to blame for the fact that she had become so fond of Jessica, the thought of ever being parted from her was like a physical pain. Not to become too emotionally involved with her charge had been part of her training, and at the kindergarten that hadn't been too difficult to do, but now…

'Has anyone ever told you that you have the most expressive eyes…?' Rufus muttered.

She gave him a startled look, suddenly feeling, as their gazes locked and held, that they were the only two people in the noisy, crowded room.

'The most amazing eyes!' he muttered again, shaking his head, as if he was under a spell he wanted broken.

'I thought you said they were expressive?' Annie murmured huskily.

'Expressive! Beautiful! Amazing…! God damn it—'

'Granny said not to use that word unless in prayer,' Jessica said reprovingly to her father—reminding the two of them that she was there! 'And you weren't praying, Daddy.' She grinned up at him teasingly.

Rufus looked down at his daughter for several stunned seconds, and then he smiled at her, lightly ruffling her hair. 'In a way, that's exactly what I was doing,' he told her softly, his expression enigmatic as he glanced across at Annie.

Annie gazed back just as enigmatically at him—because she didn't understand him at all! One minute they had been discussing the fact that she had gone very quiet, the next— Her eyes…? There seemed to be no connection between the two to Annie.

'I prayed last night too, Daddy.' Jessica continued the conversation, taking it at its face value. 'I prayed you wouldn't go away again for a very long time. What were you praying for?' she added guilelessly, completely unaware of the heart-wrenching effect her words had had on both adults.

Annie now felt even more ashamed of her earlier

thoughts, and as she looked across at Rufus she wondered how he felt at learning just how upsetting his daughter found his long absences.

His face was softened with love as he looked at Jessica. 'I prayed for the same thing, love,' he told her gruffly.

Jessica nodded in that totally adult way she sometimes had. 'Perhaps if we both pray for the same thing it might happen. I prayed for a new mother for a long time, and that didn't happen. But maybe that was because I prayed on my own,' she said consideringly, wrinkling her nose up in thought, again completely unaware of the bombshell she had just dropped into the conversation. 'What do you think, Daddy?' she looked up at him, her brow furrowed.

Annie could have laughed at the totally stunned expression on Rufus's face. He'd obviously had no idea that Jessica had hungered for a new mother—and he had no idea how to respond to her either.

Annie took pity on him. 'I think the two of us should go to the ladies' room and wash our hands after that delicious meal,' she told Jessica quickly. 'It will give you a chance to show off your prowess on your crutches,' she added encouragingly as she saw the slightly rebellious look on the little girl's face.

The crutches had been supplied by the hospital on Sunday, and Jessica took great delight in using them whenever she could, especially when she had an audience, as she did in this crowded pub.

It certainly diverted Jessica's attention from a subject her father obviously found uncomfortable, to say the least; he still looked slightly bewildered as Annie stood up to accompany Jessica across the room.

'Where the hell did that come from?' he said in a low voice before Annie could move out of earshot.

She turned to him with a sympathetic smile. 'It's one of the reasons I like working with children so much; you never quite know what they are going to say next!' It was obvious Rufus certainly hadn't expected this!

'A new mother!' he repeated incredulously.

Annie's smile widened. 'I shouldn't worry about it.' She patted his arm comfortingly. 'She's obviously given up praying for that!'

'Thank God!' He gave a relieved sigh, taking a much needed swallow of his beer.

Annie's smile faded as she turned to follow Jessica. She had forgotten how disastrous his marriage to Joanne had been; no wonder he didn't find the subject of a replacement in the least funny. It obviously wasn't an experience he cared to repeat. And who could blame him…?

He seemed deep in thought on the drive back to the house, manoeuvring the black Mercedes as if on automatic, and Jessica, tired from her trip out, fell asleep in the back of the car.

Annie was glad of the brief respite to be able to think of her earlier conversation with Anthony. He hadn't seemed the same today, certainly hadn't liked her comments about his forthcoming wedding. But what was going to happen about that? Did he intend going through with the marriage? He said not, but—

'He isn't worth it, you know.' Rufus gently interrupted her reflections, the fact that he seemed to know what—whom!—her thoughts were about proving he wasn't as lost in introspection himself as she had thought he was.

Colour warmed her cheeks. 'I don't know what you mean,' she denied awkwardly.

He sighed. 'Yes, you do. I don't know how he does it.' Rufus gave an impatient shake of his head. 'But every woman that comes within twenty feet of Anthony seems to fall for his charm—such as it is! However, no matter what he may have told you, Annie, he is going to marry Davina. Celia will see that he does,' he told her gently.

Celia...? But— 'Why?' Annie was perplexed.

Rufus shrugged. 'For the reasons I've already tried to explain to you.'

Because Davina was wealthy. And Anthony had expensive tastes. It didn't seem a very good basis for a marriage to her. And it really didn't seem any of Celia's business whom her son married. Oh, it would be better for everyone if Celia approved of her son's choice of wife, but surely it was more important that Anthony approved of her!

'I don't understand.'

'You will,' Rufus assured her grimly. 'I'm just trying to make things as painless for you as possible. Or is it too late for that?' He quirked dark brows.

Was it? She didn't know. Yes, she had been charmed by Anthony from the first, flattered by his attention in the preceding weekend visits. But his arrival with Davina this last weekend had totally thrown her. Now she wasn't sure what she felt.

'I hope to God it's not, Annie,' Rufus continued harshly. 'My brother has ruined too many lives already to add you to that number!'

His own marriage was top of that list, Annie felt sure. But surely that hadn't been Anthony's fault— Was it ever…? She didn't know any more, needed time to think, to work things out in her own head.

But there was no time for thinking once they got back to the house. Jessica needed to be seen to; the two of them were to have tea together up in the nursery as there were guests coming to dinner. And thankfully Annie didn't see anything of Anthony; she needed some time to herself before she saw him again.

To her surprise Celia was still in her bedroom suite when the time came for Jessica to say goodnight to her grandmother, the older woman in her dressing-room, trying to decide what she would wear for the evening ahead.

Her hair already styled, make-up expertly applied, only her dress and shoes to be donned, at that moment wearing a peach robe over her ultra-slender body, Celia looked elegantly beautiful. It was surprising really that she hadn't remarried after her husband's death six years ago; she was certainly still an extremely attractive woman.

'Ready for bed?' She turned to greet her granddaughter, Jessica already in her pyjamas and dressing-gown. 'Is it that late already?' She looked slightly flustered at the realisation.

Annie gave the other woman a searching look as she said goodnight to her granddaughter. There were signs of strain beside Celia's eyes and mouth that she had never really noticed before, and she looked tired too, despite the rest she had just taken before dinner. Obviously having Anthony and Davina here, plus the disturbing Rufus, was proving a strain for Celia too! Only Jessica—and possibly the vacuous Davina—seemed to be unaffected by this strange family gathering.

'And what are you going to do this evening, my dear?'

Annie blinked as she realised Celia's question was addressed to her. Once Jessica was in bed, what was she going to do? Her normal routine had been totally upset since the rest of the family had arrived!

'I have some labels to sew into some of Jessica's school uniform,' she ventured. 'And then I might go and choose a book from the library, if that's all right?' She had been enthralled with the Diamond library since the day she'd come to work here. She had always been an avid reader, and after years of a shortage of available books the large room on the ground floor of the Diamond house, which was completely dedicated to their collection of literature, was like an Aladdin's cave to her.

And as her own life seemed more than a little complicated at the moment losing herself in someone else's world seemed a very attractive proposition!

Celia smiled brightly. 'An excellent idea. Feel free to go and choose a book any time you like.'

Annie looked at the older woman more closely. Perhaps it was the strain of having Rufus back, or maybe the other woman was just mellowing on better acquaintance, but Celia had actually sounded warmly friendly just then!

'Thank you,' she accepted slightly dazedly.

'And now I really must finish dressing for dinner.' The older woman stood up smoothly, patting Jessica absently on top of her dark curls. 'I'm sure Davina's mother will be wearing something beautifully elegant; she usually does!' Celia wrinkled her nose irritably as she once again began to look through her own extensive array of clothes.

Davina's mother… It was Davina's parents who were the guests for dinner this evening! No doubt so that they could all discuss wedding plans together…

Annie went mechanically through the motions of putting Jessica to bed, even managed to sew name-tags into Jessica's new winter uniform without really being aware she was performing the tedious task. Then she found herself down in the library without really knowing how she had got there, knew that Davina's parents were close by in the dining-room, having heard their car in the driveway earlier. And wedding plans were definitely on the menu!

Where did that leave Annie? Was Rufus right? Was she to have been just another of those meaningless flings Anthony seemed to have indulged in over the years? Was he just playing with her emotions while intending to marry Davina after all? He certainly hadn't been very pleased earlier when she had questioned him about his marriage to Davina…

What a mess! She had come here to work so happily, enjoyed being with Jessica, and now, because of an involvement with Anthony that should never have begun in the first place, she had put the whole thing in jeopardy. How could she carry on working here when she had made such a fool of herself over Anthony? But she didn't want to leave, had realised that only too clearly this afternoon when she'd thought of Rufus returning for good and Jessica no longer needing her.

Without really being aware that she was doing it, Annie began sobbing quietly, for what or for whom she wasn't quite sure, everything still too muddled in her mind. One thing she did know was that whatever her relationship with Anthony was—and even now she couldn't quite put a label on it!—it would have to end.

End! It had never really begun, except in her own naive head. Rufus was right: emotionally she was young and impressionable—

'I told you he wasn't worth it!'

Annie looked up sharply at the man she had just been thinking of. Rufus was very tall and dark in his black evening suit and snowy white shirt, the expression on his face, as he strode forcefully into the library and shut the door firmly behind him, just as dark and forbidding.

'He certainly isn't worth crying over,' Rufus barked as he crossed the room with long, powerful strides, pulling Annie roughly to her feet to shake her slightly. 'Stop crying, damn it!' he grated harshly, his expression fierce now.

His annoyance just made her realise exactly how stupid she had been, which just made her cry all the harder. She had believed Anthony's interest in her to be genuine, had started to fall in love with him, and now she just felt totally stupid. Young and impressionable!

'Annie!' Rufus shook her again. 'God damn it!' His voice rose at his frustration with her tears.

She did try to stop crying, was trying very hard to stop, but the fact that it was Rufus who was witnessing her humiliation just seemed to make the whole situation worse. He was her employer; what was he going to think of her for having made such an idiot of herself over a man she was rapidly coming to agree with him wasn't worth it? Perhaps Rufus would just decide to dismiss her anyway, because she was proving a damned nuisance!

She drew in several gulping breaths. 'Jessica said you shouldn't use that word unless you're praying,' she reminded him, in an attempt to ease some of the tension of the situation.

It seemed to have no effect on Rufus, his displeasure deepening. 'Damn what Jessica says,' he grated. 'And damn what Anthony has to say too. Damn the lot of them!' His hands were still tight on her arms as he looked down at her. 'Oh, to hell with it,' he growled, before his head lowered and his mouth claimed hers.

Fiercely. Possessively. Completely!

Annie was so taken by surprise that she could do nothing but remain in the hard possession of his arms as that plundering mouth continued its ravishment of hers. She had been kissed before—quite recently!—but never like this.

And then the anger seemed to go out of Rufus, his arms no longer like steel bands but holding her tenderly against him, his mouth sipping and tasting hers, causing her pulse to leap erratically as she slowly began to return his caresses, her arms moving slowly up about his shoulders as she stood on tiptoe to deepen the kiss.

It was an invitation Rufus accepted, curving her body into his now, his mouth moving erotically against hers, his tongue moving lightly over the inner softness of her lips, causing heat to course through her body.

She was tingling all over, alive with desire, never wanting this pleasure to end—

It ended abruptly as Rufus put her away from him, eyes so dark they looked black again. 'You aren't in love with Anthony, Annie,' he bit out coldly. 'You aren't in love with anyone. You wouldn't have kissed me the way you did just now if you were. So stop your damned crying and get back to doing what you're paid to do—looking after Jessica!' He turned sharply on his heel and slammed out of the room as suddenly as he had entered it.

Annie stared after him with bewildered brown eyes, her confusion—and despair—utter and complete...

CHAPTER FIVE

'WHAT the hell is going on between you and Rufus?'

Annie had just come down the stairs from the nursery with a used lunch tray, hadn't seen Anthony since their brief conversation yesterday. In fact, she hadn't seen any member of the Diamond family today except Jessica, didn't know how to face Rufus again after what had happened between them last night.

She gave Anthony a startled look now—surely he didn't know that Rufus had kissed her? And, more importantly, that she had kissed him back!

'What do you mean?' she said guardedly, holding the tray defensively in front of her as Anthony glared at her across its width.

'Put that damned tray down,' he instructed impatiently, not waiting for her to do so but wrenching it out of her hands and depositing it unceremoniously on the table that stood in the centre of the huge hallway, one of the cups falling over in its saucer with a loud clatter, although luckily nothing actually broke. Not that Anthony seemed in the least concerned that it might have, turning to her angrily. 'Rufus has just informed me that you're all off to London for a few days,' he told her accusingly.

She looked startled. 'He has…?'

'He has,' Anthony echoed uncompromisingly. 'So what's going on?'

She would like to know that herself—because it was

the first she had heard of a trip to London! Not that there was anything unusual about a nanny being expected to travel with the family; it was just that, in Rufus Diamond's case, and in view of what had happened between them last night, it was—strange. Well…the timing of it was strange.

Goodness, she was becoming flustered just at the thought of it!

'Annie!' Anthony demanded an answer from her.

And she didn't have one. She didn't know why they were going to London, or for how long; she simply knew nothing about it. 'Are you sure he said I was to go as well?'

'Positive,' Anthony confirmed grimly.

And knowing Rufus—even as little as she did—he had enjoyed telling Anthony too!

'Just what am I supposed to do while you're off in London with my brother?' Anthony snapped.

Annie's eyes widened incredulously as she looked up at him. Considering he had spent yesterday evening with his fiancée, her parents and his mother, discussing their Christmas wedding plans, he had a damned cheek even asking her that question!

'I would say,' she said carefully, 'that you'll be doing exactly what you've been doing the last five days: enjoying your holiday, at your family home, with your fiancée!' Indignation hardened her voice as she delivered that last comment.

'Oh, I see.' Anthony took a step back from her, a knowing smile on his lips. 'We're playing those sort of games, are we?' he derided.

She didn't know what *he* was doing—she had virtually given up trying to work that one out!—but she certainly wasn't into playing games of any sort. 'I've just told you that Rufus hasn't even spoken to me about this yet, so how can I possibly be playing games—of any kind?' she said exasperatedly.

Anthony studied her assessingly. 'You're angry with me because of the wedding.'

Angry? She didn't think she was at all angry about it. She had been confused, but she didn't think she was any longer, not where this man was concerned. Now, Rufus was a different matter completely...!

'Not at all,' she answered Anthony smoothly. 'I'm sure bringing the wedding forward to Christmas will all work out perfectly. Now, if you'll excuse me...?' She moved to go past him to pick up the tray, only to find he was gripping her arms. 'Anthony, you're hurting me.' And he was, too, his fingers painful on her upper arms.

'You—'

'Annie, my dear.' Celia seemed to have appeared from nowhere, moving gracefully towards them. 'I wanted to have a few words with you about this trip you're taking with Rufus to London.'

Annie had desperately been trying to release herself from Anthony's grasp, but at his mother's mention of Rufus she suddenly found herself completely free as Anthony thrust her away from him. She turned to face Celia, her gaze stubbornly averted from Anthony's accusing one. 'I really don't know anything about it yet, Celia,' she replied. 'Perhaps Rufus only means to take Jessica with him.'

'But of course he doesn't.' The other woman easily cast that idea aside. 'I was speaking to him only a few minutes ago, and he definitely said you were to go as well as Jessica.'

Well, she wished he would stop speaking to everyone else about it and actually tell *her* what was happening! It seemed that everyone else in this household knew what she was doing for the next few days, but she didn't have a clue!

Why were they going to London? Where were they staying? How long was a few days...? Because she shouldn't spend a few days—and a few nights!—anywhere with him. Even if Jessica was there too.

'You'll have a wonderful time, my dear,' Celia encouraged as she saw the reluctance in Annie's expression. 'You may even find the time to visit some of your friends while you're there.' She smiled brightly.

Annie felt, rather than saw, the glowering look Anthony cast in her direction. Obviously the thought of her meeting up with friends—in Anthony's mind, probably male friends—did not please him. Well, she did have a lot of friends in London, and some of them were male, but they weren't those sorts of male friends. And even if they were it was none of Anthony's business; he was engaged to someone else, had no right to approve or disapprove of her seeing any of her friends, male or female.

Whew—that was a change in her attitude towards him from five days ago when he had first kissed her!

But he was engaged. And with the bringing forward of the wedding, the talk last night with Davina's parents—the other woman's father actually being Anthony's boss—it seemed a foregone conclusion that the wedding would go ahead at Christmas. What role was Anthony thinking of offering her in all that? It wasn't too difficult to guess—and neither was the answer she would give him. She had been born because her mother had been involved with a man who refused to leave his wife for her, even when he knew she was expecting his child; Annie had no intention of history repeating itself!

She had been living in cloud-cuckoo-land even thinking it would be any different for her with a man like Anthony Diamond. But thank goodness she had come to her senses now. And if Rufus Diamond believed it would be any different with him then he was in for a shock too! Young and impressionable she might be, stupid she was not!

'Yes, it would be nice,' she answered Celia lightly, ignoring Anthony's scowling expression. 'I'm sure Rufus will talk to me about it eventually.' When he had stopped telling everyone else! 'Now, if you'll both excuse me, I really do have to get this tray back to the kitchen.' She picked it up and turned to leave.

'Annie—'

'Anthony, I would like to talk to you about Davina's birthday next week,' his mother told him smoothly. 'And I'm sure Annie has a lot of other things she should be doing,' she added with hard dismissal.

And obviously talking to her son wasn't one of them!

Annie had half suspected, over the last few days, from her comments and topics of conversation, that Celia had a pretty good idea of what had transpired between her son and Jessica's nanny. She was even more convinced now that Celia knew. And Rufus was right: Celia meant to see Anthony safely married to Davina.

It was just her luck that Davina herself was walking down the hallway as Annie made her way through the large house to the kitchen. Really, she wasn't having much luck today at all!

'Ah, Annie,' Davina drawled in recognition. 'I've been meaning to have a few words with you.'

Another one!

Annie gave a resigned sigh. 'If it's about going to London with Rufus then Celia and Anthony have already told me about it.'

Davina looked mildly surprised, then shook her head. 'I can assure you it has nothing to do with London or Rufus,' she rejoined frigidly. 'I have no interest in either subject.'

Until this moment Annie had thought the girl beautiful but a bit insipid characterwise, but at this moment she sensed a steel in Davina she hadn't known was there. And if she didn't want to talk about this proposed trip to London with Rufus, what did she want to talk about? Annie found herself tensing guardedly.

Davina continued to look at her with those freezing blue eyes. 'It's about Anthony—'

'There you are, Annie,' Rufus calmly interrupted as he strode towards them. 'I've been looking for you everywhere.'

Everyone else in the family seemed to have found her, so why couldn't he?

'Hello, Davina,' he greeted the other woman warmly. 'I didn't see you standing there.'

Considering that Davina was much taller than Annie, with golden hair that gleamed brightly in the autumn sunshine, how could he possibly have missed her?

Annie had been dreading this first meeting with him after they had kissed each other last night, but, in view of the intervening conversations with Celia and Anthony, now she just felt angry with him. It didn't make her feel any less irritable towards him knowing he had probably just saved her from a very uncomfortable conversation with Davina. Because she was sure now that Davina had just been about to launch into a discussion about Anthony's overfriendliness with her. Perhaps it was as well, after all, that she was going away with Rufus and Jessica…!

'Well, you've found me,' she told Rufus ungraciously, aware that she sounded as irritable as she felt, but she couldn't help it; she was feeling emotionally battered by this family.

Rufus quirked his left eyebrow in that enigmatic way that he had. 'So I have,' he murmured speculatively.

Annie blushed at the intended rebuke. 'I'm just on my way to the kitchen to deposit this tray,' she informed him flatly. 'But I'll be more than happy to talk to you as soon as I've got rid of it.' It was starting to annoy her too now that the used plates and cups reminded her of the pleasant lunch she had shared with Jessica such a short time ago; it seemed like hours ago!

Rufus nodded. 'I'll be in the library,' he told her softly.

The library! Annie felt her heart sink at his voice, her hands shaking slightly, rattling the used crockery on the tray. The library, the place where they had kissed each other so passionately, was the last place she wanted to go to speak to him!

Which was probably the very reason why he had chosen it, Annie acknowledged heavily as she finally made her way to the kitchen and passed the tray over to the cook; Rufus was nothing if not damned annoying! He was also irritating, infuriating, a thorn in everyone's side. But especially hers!

And yet she had kissed him last night, kissed him as if she really meant it.

Well, he had kissed her too—and his parting comment about getting on with the job of looking after Jessica showed he hadn't meant it at all!

And that was what was important about last night; Rufus had only kissed her to show her she wasn't seriously emotionally involved with Anthony. That was what she had to remember about it—not that she had responded!

Rufus was seated in one of the winged leather armchairs that sat at either side of the fireplace when Annie entered the room a few minutes later, a book open on his lap, glancing up at her casually as he sensed her presence in the room.

'Dickens.' He snapped the book shut, turning to put it back on the shelf. 'Not one of my favourite authors.'

Or hers, she inwardly acknowledged, not willing, at this moment in time, to outwardly agree with him on anything. But she found Dickens a little too depressing for her taste. Actually, he would probably suit her mood just now!

'You wanted to talk to me?' she prompted abruptly.

Rufus tilted his head to one side, looking at her with amusement. 'Who's rattled your cage?' he taunted.

Her mouth tightened. 'Sorry?'

'Uh-oh.' Rufus grimaced. 'It's me you're angry with, is it?'

She drew in a harsh breath. 'Why on earth should I be angry with you?'

To her chagrin, he grinned. 'I should sit down if I were you, Annie.' He indicated the chair opposite. 'Before the carpet around you explodes into flames!' he said ruefully. 'And to think I initially doubted you were a real redhead! Okay,' he encouraged once she was seated. 'Tell me what I have to apologise for, and let's just get that out of the way. Then we can move on.'

So he was a let's-sort-this-out-and-move-on sort of person. Strange, that wasn't the impression Anthony had given with regard to Rufus's wife... But perhaps that was different; there was certainly a lot of antagonism between the two men.

'Is it last night?' Rufus was watching her closely. 'Do you want me to apologise for kissing you—is that it?'

She had been hoping he wouldn't even mention the subject. But she supposed that had been just too much to hope for!

'Well, I suppose I could apologise,' Rufus said slowly, taking her silence as confirmation. 'But I really can't see the point, when I can't promise it won't happen again.' He grinned that wolfish grin as Annie gave an audible gasp. 'That certainly woke you up!' he said with satisfaction, relaxing back in the chair. 'Is it last night, Annie—?'

'No!' she denied sharply. 'I'm just— Everyone has— We're going to London,' she concluded as she realised she was rambling.

'We are,' he nodded, eyes narrowed. 'Don't you want to go?' he prompted gently.

'Yes. No.' She gave a sigh, annoyed with herself for appearing so flustered. 'Yes, of course I do,' she said.

'You just wish I had mentioned it to you before I told anyone else,' he said knowingly. 'From your mention of "everyone", I presume the rest of the family have taken great pleasure in informing you of my plans before I had a chance to talk to you about them. I only mentioned it casually over lunch, Annie,' he told her. 'I have no idea why they all took it into their heads to tell you about it.'

She did: Anthony because he was furious that she was going away with his brother, albeit as nanny to his daughter, Celia because Annie had a feeling the other woman wanted her as far removed from Anthony as possible in the immediate future, and Davina hadn't wanted to talk to her about the trip to London at all but something much more personal! In retrospect, perhaps this interlude in London was the best thing for her too!

'It doesn't matter,' she returned easily. 'I only—'

'But of course it matters, Annie,' Rufus interrupted. 'Despite what I may have said to you last night, I don't want to hurt or upset you; I think there are probably enough people in this household intent on doing that already, without my joining in!' he went on darkly. 'And for deliberately doing that last night I do apologise.' He looked across at her, his eyes that dark, fathomless blue. 'I shouldn't have made that remark to you about looking after Jessica,' he explained at her questioning look. 'I only have to see the two of you together to know that you care for Jessica very much. And that the feeling is more than reciprocated.'

Annie swallowed hard, her voice husky when she spoke. 'Thank you.'

He grinned. 'Don't mention it.'

He was incorrigible; and how could she possibly stay angry with him when he behaved so disarmingly?

'So...' She spoke firmly, determined to get this conversation back on a businesslike level. Which wasn't easy when he had told her he couldn't promise he wouldn't kiss her again!

He mustn't kiss her again. Because if he did she was

very much afraid she would respond in exactly the same way she had last night. And becoming involved with this man, the father of her charge and a man who was out of the country more than he was in it, would be more ridiculous than her infatuation with Anthony had been!

'When do we leave?' she asked briskly. 'I'll need to get some things together for Jessica and myself.'

'We're leaving later this afternoon. And don't worry about too much for Jess; she already has quite a lot of clothes at my apartment,' Rufus replied.

His apartment! She had assumed they would be staying at a hotel...

Rather a stupid assumption for her to have made when Rufus was obviously based in London for his job. But his apartment...!

'Don't worry, Annie,' he teased at her woebegone expression. 'It has four bedrooms, so I won't be expecting you to share mine!'

God, was she so transparent? Not that she had expected to share his bedroom—he was just being deliberately mischievous now!—but she did find the thought of going to stay in his home, even with Jessica present, more than a little disturbing.

'Jessica's would have been the more obvious choice,' she told him calmly.

His mouth twisted. 'But not half as much fun!'

She gave him a look, not taking him seriously for a moment; he was obviously enjoying toying with her. And it was time it stopped. 'I had better go and get my things together, then.' She stood up to leave.

'Just enough for a few days,' Rufus warned. 'We are coming back.'

'Don't worry, Rufus.' She smiled at the almost panicked expression on his face. 'I brought all my worldly possessions down here in one large suitcase; I really won't pack that much for two or three days!'

He looked relieved to hear it. 'At last, a woman who knows not to pack the kitchen sink, along with everything else in the house!'

She laughed, giving a wry shake of her head as she crossed the room to the door.

'There is one thing, though, Annie.' The tone of Rufus's voice stopped her at the door. 'Do pack the black dress,' he told her gruffly as she slowly turned to face him.

Her eyes widened. 'Will we be going out in the evenings?'

He met her gaze unblinkingly. 'Probably not,' he returned. 'But pack the black dress anyway.'

She gave him a reproving look as she left, no longer sure whether he was serious or still playing with her. He had seemed angry last night when he had kissed her, but a night's sleep seemed to have changed all that—

'Annie!'

She frowned as she turned to see Anthony standing in the doorway of his mother's private sitting-room, that frown deepening as he beckoned to her to join him. God, she hoped Celia and Davina weren't in there too, so that all three of them could tell her how she was wasting her time over Anthony; that was all she needed on top of her puzzlement concerning Rufus. Besides, they could save their breath if that was their intention; she was cured of her infatuation with Anthony!

'Come in here, Annie,' he commanded. 'I want to talk to you.'

There was no one else in the room, she discovered

when she reluctantly entered it. Although that didn't mean Celia wouldn't arrive at any moment—

'My mother is upstairs resting.' Anthony instantly dispelled that thought as he closed the door firmly behind them.

In that case he had chosen the perfect place for them to talk in private; usually no one else but Celia entered this room, not unless she had invited them in. Celia seemed to be resting rather a lot recently... Unless it was just her way of keeping out of Rufus's path!

'What is it, Anthony?' Annie looked at him, feeling unsettled. 'I was on my way upstairs to pack for this trip to London.'

He scowled darkly. 'You're going with Rufus, then.' It was an accusation, not a question.

'I'm accompanying Jessica, yes,' she answered carefully.

'You're going with Rufus,' he repeated.

She bristled at the accusing tone in his voice. 'And you're staying here with Davina,' she reminded him tautly.

He looked at her consideringly. 'That really bothers you, doesn't it?' he said.

Of course it bothered her; he was an engaged man. And he acted as if he owned her, which, apart from being unacceptable, was a very strange experience for someone who had been on her own all her life.

'I think...' she spoke slowly '...that you need to get your life in order, Anthony.'

'In what way?' He was unsure.

'In every way!' she said exasperatedly. 'A few days ago you kissed me, then a couple of days later you made an assignation to meet me down on the jetty. Admittedly you didn't get there,' she continued determinedly as she could see he was about to interrupt her, 'but that was only because your fiancée wanted your time instead. Which she has a perfect right to expect. Now, correct me if I'm wrong,' she went on scathingly, 'but this engagement, which you tell me is such a sham, now seems to have progressed to discussing Christmas wedding arrangements. In view of that, I'm not really sure where you think I fit into all this!' Her eyes flashed deeply brown with her barely contained anger.

'Rufus was right, you know.' Anthony looked at her admiringly. 'You really are rather beautiful when you're angry!'

She gave him an indignant glance, stepping back as he would have moved towards her. 'I believe Rufus merely commented on the fact that I was obviously a true redhead.' She knew exactly what he had said—and the word 'beautiful' had never been used!

'Whatever,' Anthony responded carelessly, his smile full of charm. 'I think you look beautiful when you're angry. Except—' now he did move a step closer, mere inches away from Annie '—I'm not sure I like you being angry with me,' he added tenderly, reaching out to lightly grasp her arms. 'Lighten up, Annie,' he encouraged soothingly as he sensed her resistance. 'We could have a lot of fun together if you would just relax a bit.'

Fun! This hadn't been fun so far; she had been mortified, and then guilt-stricken, that she had kissed—and allowed herself to be kissed by—a man engaged to another woman. And Anthony called this having fun! Well, he could have it without her!

'Until your wedding at Christmas,' she rebutted, pulling away from him.

'And after—if things work out between us. And I can't see any reason why they shouldn't.' His hands tightened painfully on her arms as she again tried to pull away from him.

Annie's eyes widened, her breathing so shallow she was barely breathing at all. 'You can't?' she bit out tautly.

'Not if you lighten up, no,' he chided easily.

Annie was barely resisting the impulse she had to punch him on his aristocratic nose—and he obviously had no idea just how vexed she was as he gave her his most disarming smile. 'If I lighten up?' she echoed slowly, the fury building up inside her.

'Exactly.' He grinned. 'Okay, so I'll have a wife, but I'll still visit here often—and I'll make sure Davina stays in London when I do.'

'You will?' Her emotions were barely contained now. Anthony was digging himself deeper and deeper into a hole that at any moment now she was going to take great pleasure in pushing him into!

'Of course,' Anthony continued unconcernedly.

'I would be your mistress?' Her hands were so tightly clenched at her sides, her nails were digging into her palms.

'It's a bit of an old-fashioned way of putting things,' he acknowledged. 'But yes, I suppose that's exactly what you would be.'

'Well, that's where you're wrong!' Her control finally snapped as she pushed him away from her, and the expression of surprise on his face at her obvious wrath would have been laughable—if she hadn't felt less like laughing than ever before in her life!

And she had thought he cared about her—had imagined the two of them together, falling in love—when all the time he was no better than her own father had been!

'I should stop right there, if I were you, Anthony— unless you have some sort of perverted desire to be the recipient of the punch on the nose I so much want to give you!' She was breathing hard in her agitation, breasts heaving, eyes blazing. 'I don't intend—ever!— being your mistress or any other man's!' And with that last furious comment she turned and slammed out of the room.

She had been right earlier. A mistress! Good God, he had chosen completely the wrong woman to offer that role in his life. She—

'Well, you certainly told him,' remarked an admiring voice.

Annie swung round to face Rufus, anger burning brightly in her cheeks as he stood leaning casually against the wall, his relaxed pose seeming to imply he had been standing there for some time. For how long? Surely he hadn't heard all—

'Sorry about that.' He straightened away from the wall. 'I was just passing, and I happened to hear the word "mistress" being used. I'm afraid I was hooked after that.' He shrugged. 'Although I'm really rather sorry you didn't punch him on the nose as you said you wanted to.' He grinned.

Annie didn't think, didn't want to think, acting instinctively as she reached out and slapped him hard across his cheek, still too angry to cry. Then she simply turned on her heel and walked away.

CHAPTER SIX

HE HADN'T followed her!

Annie hadn't stopped walking until she'd reached her bedroom, but with each step she had expected to feel Rufus's hand roughly on her arm as he turned her to face him and told her she no longer had a job looking after his daughter!

But it hadn't happened.

She had sat on her bed for the next ten minutes, waiting for him to burst into the room.

That hadn't happened either.

Why hadn't it?

She didn't know now. She had smacked Rufus for no other reason than he'd happened to be in the wrong place at the wrong time, had vented on him the anger she actually felt towards Anthony. And towards herself, if she was honest, for being so stupid, so *young and impressionable*!

Perhaps that last was partly the reason why she had hit out at Rufus—because he had been right!

Which was no excuse at all. Rufus couldn't be blamed for knowing his brother better than she did. But he had certainly paid the price for that knowledge. The evidence of it—livid red marks on his cheeks—still showed two hours later!

If Annie turned her head slightly from where she sat next to him in the front of his Mercedes, Jessica comfortably ensconced on the back seat, then she could actually see the imprint her hand had made on the hardness of his cheek.

But she tried hard not to turn her head any more, not even fractionally. In fact, she hadn't been able to do more than mutter a few words as Rufus had put her small overnight bag in the boot of the car at the beginning of their journey. She didn't want to be here at all, didn't want to draw any more attention to herself than was strictly necessary. It was bad enough that—

'I'm sorry, Annie.'

She turned sharply to face Rufus as he drove, swallowing hard as she instantly saw those marks on his cheek. Marks she had made. She had always believed herself incapable of physically hurting another human being, and yet looking at Rufus she could see what she had done to him. And he was apologising to her! What on earth for?

He reached out with one hand and lightly squeezed both her hands as they lay tightly clenched together in her lap. 'Anthony is a bastard,' he said tightly, his eyes focused on the road ahead.

Annie glanced quickly round at Jessica, relieved to see the girl was fast asleep.

'She hates long journeys,' Rufus said, looking at his daughter in the driver's mirror, as Annie faced back to the front once again. He released his hold on her hands. 'Sleep is her way of avoiding them,' he explained indulgently.

Annie wished she could fall asleep too, wished today had never happened! 'I'm sorry I hit you—'

'Hey,' he chided softly. 'I've just been trying to tell you that I deserved it—'

'Not you.' She shook her head firmly.

'Believe me—' he grimaced ruefully '—that isn't the first punch I've taken for Anthony.'

'It will be the last from me.' She shivered with re-action at what she had done.

Rufus ran a hand over his bruised cheek, while his other gripped the steering wheel. 'That's quite a pow-erful right you have there, Miss Fletcher—'

'Please don't,' she groaned, tears of contrition flood-ing her eyes now. 'I'm so ashamed. Can't believe I really did that.' She shook her head, the tears wet on her cheeks. 'You must—'

'I mustn't anything, Annie,' he cut in gently. 'You were hurting, and the best way to get rid of some of that hurt was to—'

'Hit you!' She groaned again, burying her face in her hands, crying in earnest now. Which was all she seemed to have done just recently!

'Aw, Annie, don't cry!' Rufus moaned protestingly. 'I can't stand it when you cry. Especially over someone like Anthony.' His voice had hardened. 'Annie, stop it!' he instructed harshly as he gathered her up into his arms.

It was the first indication she had that he had stopped the car, and she raised her head to look around them dazedly, realising as she did so that Rufus had pulled the car over onto the hard shoulder and parked there. Something that was completely illegal, unless it was an emergency—

'This is an emergency, Annie,' he stated, and Annie realised she must have spoken the words out loud.

Then, as his mouth came forcefully down on hers, she wasn't thinking at all, only feeling.

And was she feeling! She had never known anything

like this searing pleasure she found in his arms, never felt this heat in her body, a need for more, for—

'Are we there, Daddy?'

It was as if Rufus and Annie had received an electric shock as they simultaneously registered the sleepy sound of Jessica's voice from the back of the car. They moved quickly apart, Annie more flustered now than she had been a few minutes ago. Every time this man kissed her she responded unrestrainedly. She hardly knew herself!

'Annie—'

'Daddy, are we there?' Jessica's voice rose querulously as she received no response to her first question.

Rufus gave Annie a look before turning in his seat to look at his daughter. 'No, Jess, we aren't there yet—'

'Then why have we stopped?' Jessica persisted, totally disorientated as she looked around her.

Annie returned Rufus's gaze helplessly as he looked back at her for assistance; they could hardly tell the little girl the truth!

'Er—well—Annie had something in her eye!' Rufus finally burst out awkwardly, giving Annie a censorious glare as she tried to hold back her laughter.

Something in her eye, indeed. Mud, probably!

She had allowed Rufus to kiss her again. Last night he had kissed her because he was angry. And she was upset. Today he had kissed her because he felt sorry for her. Because she was upset. The common factor to both incidents seemed to have been her tears. Then she would just have to make sure she didn't cry again! In his presence, anyway...

'Is it better now?' Jessica, thankfully, was still sleepy.

Rufus gave Annie a mocking glance. 'Is it better now?' he teased softly. 'Did I kiss it better?'

She gave him a frowning look before turning to Jessica. 'I'm much better now, thank you. So much better, in fact—'

'Oh, hell!' Rufus muttered with feeling, watching the driving mirror in front of him.

Annie looked at him in alarm. 'What is it?' she prompted in a puzzled voice. 'Rufus?'

He shook his head. 'The trouble you've caused me, woman!' Even as he spoke he was thrusting open the car door next to him. 'I find it difficult to believe I've only known you forty-eight hours!' He swung easily out of the car.

Annie turned just in time to see a policeman approaching the Mercedes, a brightly marked police car parked a short distance behind them. Their having stopped here was, as she had already surmised, illegal. And she very much doubted that the policeman would accept the story of there having been something in the eye of the lady passenger in Rufus's car. Rufus was right: she was nothing but trouble!

Jessica scrambled up into a sitting position, looking out of the back window. 'Has Daddy done something wrong?' Her voice sounded slightly awed. 'Is he going to get told off?'

She hoped not—or she would never hear the end of it!

The two men continued to talk on the roadside for several minutes, and Annie's heart sank with dismay as the young policeman took his notebook out of his pocket and began to take notes. He was booking Rufus! And it was all her fault. Rufus was going to be furious with her this time, no doubt about it.

She inwardly prepared herself for his blistering attack

as he parted from the policeman, a folded piece of paper in his hand as he walked briskly back to the car, his expression grim. There wasn't going to be any kissing better this time—even if she was upset!

She wasn't sure whether she was relieved or sad about that…

And she really didn't have the time to dwell on the subject as Rufus got back into the car beside her.

'Daddy—'

'Not yet, pumpkin,' Rufus told his daughter tautly, glancing in his driving mirror. 'I need to get us back onto the road as soon as possible.' He switched on the engine, put the car into gear, and very neatly manoeuvred the vehicle back into the swift flow of traffic.

Annie didn't know what to say, wasn't sure she should say anything; it might just make matters worse. If that were possible!

'A bit of luck, that.' Rufus was finally the one to break the silence, sitting back more comfortably in his seat now that they were well away from the police car.

'Luck?' Annie echoed incredulously; it was the last description she would have applied to the encounter!

'Mmm.' Rufus gave her a brief grin. 'The policeman recognised my name, and it seems he's a fan of mine. He particularly liked a piece I wrote last year about suburban crime; his brother, another policeman—it seems to run in the family!—was mentioned in it quite favourably. Apparently he meant to keep the article, but his wife unwittingly used that newspaper to light the fire; he asked if I could send him a copy. I've got it on disk somewhere in the flat, so I'll look it out for him when we get there.'

The piece of paper Rufus had been given wasn't a

ticket at all, but the policeman's address. And she had been imagining all sorts of horrors—charges, court appearances…!

'So there are some benefits to being famous,' she said tartly.

Rufus glanced at her again briefly. 'I'm not famous, Annie,' he finally said slowly.

'But your work is,' she challenged, not really sure why she was so angry, only that she was!

'Perhaps.' He shrugged dismissively. 'What the hell? It saved us from a severe reprimand. He just laughed when I told him I'd stopped because you had something in your eye!' Rufus reached out and squeezed her hand again, conspiratorially this time, before replacing his own hand on the wheel.

'Shall I go back to sleep for a while, Daddy?' Jessica spoke again from behind them.

Reminding Annie of exactly what she was doing here! She was here as Jessica's nanny, was here on sufferance, had no right to be angry—about anything.

'If you like, pumpkin.' Rufus answered his daughter absently. 'We'll be a while yet.'

Jessica gave a weary sigh as she settled down again on the back seat, and Annie could have sighed along with her; they hadn't even reached London yet, and she was already wishing she weren't here! How on earth was she supposed to share an apartment with this man for the next few days, even with Jessica present…?

'You've gone very quiet,' Rufus remarked a few minutes later.

She looked across at him. 'Have I?' she said guardedly—because on her guard was how she was going to have to be with this man in the future!

'You know you have,' he bit out impatiently.

Annie let out a breath. 'I don't believe I've ever been a chatterbox.'

'I didn't say that's what you are, you just— Damn it woman,' he snapped irritably. 'I never know whether to kiss you or shake you when you annoy me like this!'

She swallowed hard. 'In future I suggest you stick to shaking me—it's probably safer for everyone!'

Rufus threw her a stunned glance, and then he threw back his head with that now familiar shout of laughter. 'You, young lady, are not good for my ego,' he explained once his amusement had abated.

Her own mouth quirked with laughter in spite of herself, her bad humour of a few minutes ago totally dispelled. 'It wasn't your ego I was thinking of,' she taunted lightly. 'The next policeman may not be a fan of yours!'

'True,' he agreed dryly. 'But the onus is on you not to do anything that will make me want to kiss or shake you!'

She wasn't quite sure, at the moment, how she was supposed to do that; if she spoke she seemed to say the wrong thing, and if she didn't speak that seemed to be wrong too!

The safest thing to do seemed to be to join Jessica—and go to sleep!

She closed her eyes, feigning tiredness, and very soon she wasn't pretending at all, but genuinely asleep...

It was dark by the time they entered London, and, having just woken up, it was a minute or two before Annie realised in which part of the city they were. It wasn't one she was too familiar with, Mayfair being an area she had only passed through in the past. But she wasn't at all surprised when Rufus turned the black Mercedes down into an underground car park situated beneath a prestigious apartment building; he effectively owned Clifftop House and all the land around it, so it stood to reason that his London home would be just as prestigious.

She wasn't surprised by the security of the building, either, a guard situated in the car park itself, another one in the lobby upstairs. Not that the men challenged their progress at all, obviously recognising Rufus as one of the wealthy tenants. The apartment itself didn't actually seem like part of a block, being on the ground floor, with its own high-walled garden at the rear.

It was beautifully furnished, too, with obviously genuine antique furniture, the carpets in muted golds and greens. Elegance was the word that came to mind as Annie looked around. It was a far cry from the minute flat she had shared with three other girls until a short time ago; the huge sitting-room was almost as big as their whole accommodation had been!

'I only rent it, Annie.' Rufus was watching her reaction to her surroundings. 'I don't own it.'

The monthly rent on a place like this would probably amount to almost a year's wages for her!

'God damn it!' Rufus suddenly ground out. 'I've never had to apologise for my choice of home before!'

It wasn't his home that bothered her—given the choice she would probably have gone for somewhere like this herself! No, it was the location and obvious cost of it that overwhelmed her, and emphasised the gulf between her own lifestyle and that of the Diamond family. But she certainly wasn't asking him to apologise for it!

'It's very nice,' she told him stiltedly, swallowing hard as he just looked even more annoyed. And they both knew what happened when he became annoyed!

'It's very tidy,' Jessica put in. 'You obviously haven't been home for a while, Daddy,' she added mischievously.

'Not at all in the last three months,' he acknowledged wearily. 'I submitted my last story when I arrived in England on Wednesday, and came straight down to Clifftop House.'

Annie frowned across at him; he had been in a hurry to get there...

To see Jessica? Or had it been something else that had brought him so quickly to the family home?

He returned her questioning gaze enigmatically, and Annie knew she would find no answers there, not unless Rufus was prepared to give her them. He didn't look as if he was!

'I did, however, have some supplies brought in earlier today,' Rufus continued briskly. 'So it's a cup of tea for Annie and myself, and a juice for you, young lady.' He ruffled Jessica's hair affectionately. 'You show Annie to the bedroom next to yours, Jess, and I'll go and make the drinks.'

Annie was glad of these few minutes' respite, if only to accustom herself to her new surroundings. She should have realised that Rufus's apartment wouldn't be anything like the rooms in the old Victorian house that had been her own home until two months ago. He was a Diamond, came from a very wealthy family. She should have expected this.

It was proof of just how lacking in professionalism their relationship had become that she hadn't expected this. She made Rufus laugh, made him angry, annoyed him, and in the last twenty-four hours he had kissed her, twice. She had almost forgotten they were employer and employee. She mustn't forget again.

'It's a lovely room,' she told Jessica once the young girl had shown her to the bedroom she had been allocated. And it *was* a lovely room, the gold and cream decor making it appear warm and welcoming. But it didn't really matter whether it was a lovely room or not; she would only be occupying it for a short time!

'It's ages since Daddy brought me here,' Jessica told her wistfully.

So the trip to London wasn't a regular occurrence; Annie couldn't help wondering what had prompted it this time...

She smiled at Jessica. 'Perhaps twisting your ankle wasn't such a bad thing, after all,' she teased.

Jessica grinned back at her, a grin that was so like her father's. For the first time Annie found herself wondering what Joanne had looked like. There were no pictures of Jessica's mother at Clifftop House, and she had only noticed a large framed photograph of Jessica in the sitting-room here. One thing Annie was pretty sure of: Joanne wouldn't have been a short redhead!

Now that was a strange thought to have come into her head...

'Let's go and have our drinks,' Jessica prompted. 'Daddy isn't very domesticated,' she confided. 'So the tea will probably be awful!'

They were still laughing together over this as they entered the kitchen a few seconds later.

'Care to share the joke?' Rufus invited indulgently as he stood across the room pouring the tea.

Annie looked at Jessica, Jessica looked at Annie, and they both shook their heads at the same time, causing them to burst into laughter once again. In fact, it felt good to Annie to be able to laugh; there had been so little to laugh at just recently.

'Oh, I see.' Rufus nodded knowingly. 'I'm the brunt of it!' he accepted as he handed Annie her cup of tea.

The sight of the tea set the two of them off into peals of laughter once again, so much so that Annie couldn't take the cup from Rufus for fear of dropping it.

'Oh, I understand—it's the tea that caused the laughter in the first place!' He put the cup down, peering down into it. 'I must admit, it does look pretty awful.' He grimaced.

'That's exactly how I said it would look!' Jessica still giggled. 'Why do you think I always prefer to drink juice when I'm here?'

'You little monkey!' Her father gave her an imaginary cuff about the ear. 'I suppose you think Annie can do better?' he challenged.

Annie's eyes widened. 'I wasn't the one disparaging your tea-making skills!'

'No—but you were laughing at them,' he instantly returned.

Annie took a tentative look into the cup he had been about to give her, her distaste instinctive as she saw the mud-coloured fluid. 'How many teabags did you put in the pot?' she asked incredulously.

'I like strong tea,' he defended dryly.

'So do I,' she replied. 'But—I was always told "one for each person, and one for the pot".' She looked at him questioningly.

'It's a big pot,' he muttered grudgingly.

Annie looked at him knowingly. 'How many teabags did you use?' she persisted.

'Enough,' he muttered again.

'Daddy!' Jessica scolded him lightly. 'You're pre-prevar—'

'Prevaricating,' he finished irritably. 'Okay, six. I put six teabags in the pot!' He glared at them both.

Annie bit her lip to stop herself from laughing again, saying nothing more, and went to empty the teapot and start again. At least he had managed to warm the pot for her! 'Would you care for tea, too, Jessica?' She held a fourth teabag over the pot.

'Don't you dare say yes, just because I haven't made it,' her father warned. 'I'll be in the lounge when you've made the tea.'

Annie watched him leave the room, her mouth still twitching with laughter. 'Do you think we've hurt his feelings?' she murmured to Jessica.

'No.' The little girl made herself comfortable on one of the stools that stood in front of the breakfast-bar. 'He'll probably be glad to have a decent cup of tea himself for a change!'

Annie didn't know whether he was or not when they joined him in the lounge, Rufus taking the cup of tea from her without saying a word. But it wasn't an uncomfortable silence, and on reflection Annie had to admit she had enjoyed the exchange in the kitchen. They might have been a real family—

She pulled her thoughts up sharply. Families were for other people, not her. One day she might have a family of her own, but until then she must guard against becoming too attached to Jessica. And her father...!

Rufus made her laugh. She had never really been able

to do that with a man before. And that laughter was even more heady than his kisses had been. Dangerous territory, she realised that. Because Rufus wasn't the marrying kind. He loved his daughter, that much was obvious, and no doubt there had been women in his life since his wife died, but his choice of career didn't allow for any permanent relationships. And he already knew, from the conversation he had overheard between herself and Anthony, her views on mistresses—

She brought her thoughts up sharp once again. What on earth was she thinking of? The man had kissed her twice, not declared undying love for her. Or anything else, for that matter!

'Very nice.' Rufus put his empty cup down.

'Daddy!' Jessica reproved him once again.

'I said it was nice, didn't I?' he retorted irritably. 'Can you cook too?' He turned to Annie, his expression hopeful.

'Please say you can!' Jessica looked at her imploringly.

She hadn't thought about it before, had become used, over the last couple of months, she realised, to the fact that there was a cook in residence at Clifftop House to prepare the meals for everyone. But this was a bachelor apartment, had none of those niceties…

She nodded. 'Just basic stuff, you understand,' she explained hastily; cordon bleu she was not!

'Daddy can't even boil an egg,' Jessica confided candidly.

'I can so,' he instantly protested, but there was laughter dancing in his eyes.

'No, you can't,' his daughter contradicted him. 'Remember that time you—?'

'Okay, okay.' Rufus held up his hands defensively. 'I can't cook,' he conceded wearily.

'He forgot to put any water in the saucepan,' Jessica told Annie in a whisper deliberately loud enough for her father to hear. 'I don't know if you've ever seen an egg explode, but—'

'No, Jessica, I haven't, although I'm sure it's very—interesting,' Annie cut in swiftly as she could see Rufus was going to be the one to explode if this maligning of his culinary skills went on much longer. 'Now I know the real reason the two of you wanted me along on this trip!' she added with mock indignation. 'You just didn't want to risk your father's cooking—or to starve!'

'She's sussed us out, Jess.' Rufus winked at his daughter conspiratorially.

'It wasn't too difficult,' Annie returned witheringly. 'So what are we having to eat this evening?' She arched questioning brows, sure he had had the food for their evening meal delivered today too.

'Steak and salad,' Rufus answered instantly. 'But Jess and I can do the salad—'

'I'll do it, Daddy,' Jessica cut in firmly, turning to Annie. 'The last time Daddy made the salad I found a slug in my—'

'Okay, I'll leave you two girls to get dinner.' Rufus stood up decisively. 'I have some calls to catch up on, anyway. I'll be in my study—first door on the right out of here—when it's ready.' He strode purposefully out of the room.

Annie turned to Jessica, a smile curving her lips. 'I think we drove him away with our teasing!'

'Don't you believe it; he was glad to escape.' Jessica

shrugged dismissively, starting to help with the preparations for dinner.

It was a happy half-hour, Annie concentrating on seasoning and grilling the steaks she had found so conveniently in the refrigerator, while Jessica hobbled about preparing the salad. They laid the table between the two of them once the steaks were sizzling away, Annie having found a French loaf to accompany the meal too. It all looked very appetising once it was put on the kitchen table, Annie having opted for this casual comfort rather than the formal dining-room she had seen earlier, anxious that Jessica did not put too much strain on her slowly healing ankle.

'Not bad.' Annie nodded her satisfaction with the meal they had put out on the table. 'Even if I do say so myself.'

'I'll go and get Daddy.' Jessica was eager to show him their handiwork.

'I'll go,' Annie told her firmly. 'You've done enough walking on that ankle for one evening.'

'Can I light the candles, then?'' Jessica prompted eagerly.

Annie turned at the door. 'Not until I come back with your father. And if he says yes, then you can.'

The candles had been Jessica's idea, as had the two wineglasses for herself and Rufus; Jessica had assured her that her father would want wine with his meal. Annie wasn't sure whether he would or not, but she was happy to go along with it, although one glass of wine was her own personal limit; any more than that and she was apt to get silly.

She could hear Rufus talking on the telephone as she approached his study, hesitating outside the door as she wondered if she should interrupt him. But she didn't want their meal to ruin either, and—

She became suddenly still, actually about to knock on the door, when she unwittingly heard part of his conversation.

'Please ask Margaret to call me when she gets in.' Rufus spoke firmly. 'I really need to talk to her.'

Margaret...? There was only one Margaret that Annie knew of who had come into the conversation recently, and that was her predecessor.

Rufus was in contact with Margaret. And he really needed to talk to her...

Why? Oh, Annie accepted that the other woman had left without notice, but even so—

'Yes, I received her letter.' Rufus was still talking to the other person on the end of the telephone line. 'But I still need to talk to Margaret herself.'

The other woman had written to him! They were on close terms...?

Was Anthony not the only member of the Diamond family who had a penchant for the servants...?

CHAPTER SEVEN

'YOU were very quiet during dinner,' Rufus remarked.
The two of them were in the sitting-room, Jessica safely
in bed.

Annie was surprised she had even been able to eat the
meal, with each mouthful threatening to choke her! And
as for her personal limit of one glass of wine—! She
had accepted every refill of the red wine that Rufus had
offered her, her thoughts tumbling over each other in
their haste to be considered.

Rufus and Margaret...

So many things had fallen into place now. Rufus had
seemed very upset at finding the other woman was no
longer at Clifftop House, had questioned everyone as to
the possible reason for her abrupt departure. And he had
wasted no time in coming back to London once he'd
realised that was where she must be. Obviously so that
he could speak to her in person.

Perhaps the two of them had had a row, or maybe
Margaret had just decided the relationship wasn't for her
after all. Whatever her reasons, Rufus desperately
wanted to see her again.

Annie had got through dinner in miserable silence,
hardly able to believe her stupidity. She hadn't fallen for
the wrong man once, but twice, and within days of each
other! How naive could she be? Anthony, she had
quickly realised, had been a terrible mistake on her part,
but Rufus—! Rufus was something else entirely... He

was tall and strong, honest and dependable—hah, dependable!—or so she had thought until a short time ago.

She had been falling in love with him, she had realised as she'd stood numbly on the other side of his study door.

She had enjoyed being in his company, felt she could relax and be herself with him, while at the same time feeling completely challenged by him. And he made her laugh...

Well, she wasn't laughing now. And she hadn't laughed through dinner, either. It was as if all the friendly banter and teasing that had preceded the meal had never been; dinner had just been something she had to get through.

But she had got through it, had accepted with a bright, meaningless smile the compliments about her cooking, had seen Jessica settled into bed while Rufus cleared away—something Jessica had assured her he *could* do!

Now all Annie wanted to do was escape to her own bedroom and lick her wounds in private. And to her dismay there were wounds, her mistake where Rufus was concerned hurting her deeply.

'Annie?' Rufus prompted in a puzzled voice at her lack of response to his comment.

She stood up abruptly, her hands clasped tightly together to stop their trembling. 'I'm very tired. I think I'll go to bed too, if you don't mind?' To her chagrin, she couldn't even look at him, talking to a spot somewhere over his left shoulder as he sat in one of the armchairs.

'You haven't even touched the brandy I poured for you,' he pointed out mildly.

And rightly so—any more alcohol and she was likely to fall over!

Had he entertained Margaret here too, with or without Jessica present? Had he poured Margaret brandy after dinner and expected her to sit in here and drink it with him? Was that how it had all started? Had the two of them—?

'Annie, you don't look too well.' Rufus stood up, putting his brandy glass down on the table before crossing the room to her side. 'A few seconds ago your face was flushed; now you've gone deathly white.' He looked at her worriedly.

A few seconds ago she had been flushed from the wine she had drunk, and now she had gone white because she was going to be sick!

She turned quickly and ran from the room, just getting to the bathroom before she was violently ill, bringing up all the food she had so painstakingly forced down her throat such a short time ago, her eyes watering from the suddenness of the attack. Rufus came in behind her.

'You really aren't well, are you?' he said soothingly, pressing a damp cloth to her forehead.

His presence in the bathroom only succeeded in making her feel more ill. She should just die right now, just lie down and—

'Come on, I'll help you to your bedroom,' Rufus told her indulgently, still keeping the cloth pressed against her forehead.

Annie straightened, flushing away the evidence of her illness as she did so. 'No!' she said sharply. 'Really. I'm fine.' She pushed the cloth away, relieved to see her hand was shaking only slightly. 'I've never been a good traveller,' she said by way of an excuse. 'It was probably that that made me ill.'

'Motion sickness.' Rufus nodded understandingly.

More like *emotion* sickness! 'Something like that,' she agreed, just wanting the privacy of her bedroom now, sure she must look a sight.

'Horses and cars,' Rufus said dryly. 'You don't have a lot of luck, do you?'

Especially where men were concerned, she inwardly groaned. And they were conducting this conversation in the bathroom, of all places!

'Not a lot,' she acknowledged weakly, sidestepping out of the room.

Rufus followed her out into the hallway. 'Do you remember the way to your bedroom? I didn't know if you had a geographical problem, too,' he added at her puzzled expression.

Annie sensed that he was laughing at her, although she could tell nothing from his expression as he met her gaze with that left brow raised enigmatically. That was enough in itself to tell her he was indeed mocking her.

'No, only horses and cars,' she snapped. 'I'll feel better in the morning.' She would make sure that she did! A severe self-talking-to was what she needed. And it was what she was going to get, too! 'If you'll excuse me…?' She turned in the direction of the bedroom she would be occupying during her stay here.

'Annie?'

She stopped as Rufus softly called her name, turning reluctantly to look at him. 'Yes?' she said warily.

He looked so handsome standing there, still wearing the black shirt and blue denims he had worn for the drive down here—he hadn't had time to change before eating, after concluding his telephone call. To Margaret...

He grinned that heart-stopping grin. 'Goodnight,' he said.

'Goodnight,' she returned abruptly, turning quickly now and making good her escape before he could delay her any further.

She checked on Jessica before going to bed herself. The little girl was fast asleep, curled up into a ball in the bed, a half-smile of contentment on her lips. The sleep of the innocent...

Well, *she*, Annie, was still an innocent too, she decided once she reached the privacy of her bedroom. She should have realised Rufus's concern over Margaret's departure had been too extreme to be about the simple leaving of an employee. Even Anthony, completely self-centred as he was, had questioned Rufus's interest in it.

Rufus and the unknown Margaret...

Oh, she had realised that Rufus would have been involved with other women since his wife died; he was too virile a man for it to be any other way. Especially if, as Anthony had implied, he and Joanne hadn't been particularly happy together. But Annie just hadn't realised Jessica's previous nanny had been one of those women. And from the way Rufus was still pursuing Margaret it was far from over as far as he was concerned!

The laughter, the banter, the kisses that they had shared—all meant nothing. Not to Rufus, anyway...

As far as her own feelings were concerned, the sooner Rufus disappeared on another assignment the better!

If he wasn't around, a constant reminder of the feelings she had for him, then surely, with time, she would get over him?

She certainly hoped so! In fact, she was determined that she would. From tomorrow morning onwards she would make sure their relationship stayed strictly within the boundaries of employer and employee.

That decision made, she fell asleep. Maybe not as innocently and trouble-free as Jessica, but she was so tired that she did sleep.

She had overslept!

The clock face on the bedside radio alarm read nine-fifteen! She couldn't remember the last time she had slept as late as this. What on earth was Rufus going to think of her tardiness? At this rate she was going to be sacked!

She dressed hurriedly in denims and a burnt-orange-coloured jumper, the latter making her hair appear an even deeper red than usual. There was no time for any make-up, and she only ran her brush quickly through her hair before hurrying out to the kitchen. Jessica would be wanting her breakfast, Rufus too, if last night's description of his culinary skills was anything to go by. They would—

The large piece of paper attached by a magnet to the front of the refrigerator door read, 'I've taken Jessica to the park. Help yourself to breakfast. Hope you slept well.' It was signed 'Rufus'.

Annie sat down abruptly at the kitchen table; all her haste had been unnecessary. Jessica wasn't even here to be looked after. Annie wasn't altogether sure that last remark on Rufus's note, about sleeping well, wasn't sarcastic...

She found herself looking down at the piece of paper, which she had taken down from the fridge door. It was the first time she had seen Rufus's handwriting, and she found herself studying it. It was large and strong, the R at the beginning of Rufus written with a flourish. It was rather like the man himself, big and slightly overwhelming, larger than life.

The apartment seemed very empty without him in it. And Jessica too, of course. But it was Rufus she really missed. He had only gone to the park and she missed him. And last night she had decided the sooner he went away the better!

She groaned, burying her face in her hands. She was in love with Rufus!

What she had felt towards Anthony was nothing compared to the emotions surging through her for Rufus. And he was just as out of reach as Anthony had been, also had another woman in his life—

She almost fell off the chair in surprise as the telephone on the kitchen wall began to ring!

She simply looked at it for several seconds; should she answer it or not? It was Rufus's telephone, and the call would obviously be for him. But it could be an emergency. It could even be Rufus himself, telephoning because something had happened to Jessica.

She had to answer it!

'Rufus Diamond's residence.' She spoke stiltedly into the mouthpiece, tightly gripping the receiver to her ear.

There was silence on the other end of the line for several awkward seconds, telling Annie that the caller was as stunned to hear a female voice on the line as Annie had been reluctant to answer the call at all!

'Could I talk to Rufus, please?' The accent was Irish, the voice slightly husky—and definitely female.

Which only increased Annie's nervousness. Surely this wasn't another one? Rufus gave such an impression of being relaxed with himself and confident, but surely he couldn't be that relaxed or confident if there were a number of different women in his life? What if they all decided to turn up at his apartment at the same time? What if, like now, one of those women answered a call from one of the others…?

'Er—not at the moment,' Annie answered evasively, not at all comfortable with this conversation. 'He's taken Jessica to the park.' Surely it was all right to mention Rufus's daughter? Although, from the way he usually lived here alone, a lot of people probably didn't even know he had a daughter. Maybe this woman didn't know—

'How is she?' The woman's voice softened affectionately as she spoke of the little girl.

Not only did this woman know of Jessica, she had obviously met her!

'Very well,' Annie answered sharply—she registered the slightly possessive note in her own voice. But she couldn't help the way she felt, both Jessica and Rufus having become so very important to her.

'That's good,' the woman returned just as briskly. 'And would you be the housekeeper?'

Annie bristled. 'No, I wouldn't be the housekeeper,' she answered quickly, at the same time having no intention of saying who she was. 'Can I take a message?' she offered abruptly.

'If you wouldn't mind,' the woman accepted mildly,

telling Annie her resentment had been felt—and reacted to.

She sighed. 'No, I wouldn't mind.'

'Would you tell Rufus that Margaret called? That I'll be at home for the rest of the day if he would like to call me back when he gets in?'

Annie barely heard the last bit of the message; the name Margaret was the only thing that had really registered. This was Jessica's ex-nanny, the woman Rufus had tried so desperately to talk to the evening before?

She swallowed hard. 'I'll tell him.'

'Thank you,' Margaret returned gratefully. 'And say hello to Jessica for me, and give her my love,' she added before ringing off.

Annie sat down again. She didn't want to give Rufus the message. And she didn't want to pass on Margaret's love to Jessica, either!

Which was ridiculous. If she didn't tell Rufus about the call, so that he couldn't return it, then Margaret was sure to telephone again. And then Annie would look a complete fool for not telling him Margaret had called this morning while he was out! But she wasn't even sure she could say the words, thought they might possibly choke her!

She could always write it down, and just hand the message to Rufus... The piece of paper on which he had written his note to her was still on the kitchen table...

Coward, she admonished herself as she hastily scribbled Margaret's message down. But she couldn't help that; with her own newly recognised feelings for Rufus, to tell him of another woman's telephone call would hurt her deeply.

After writing down the message she busied herself

unstacking the dishwasher, filled with crockery from dinner last night, had almost finished putting the things away in the cupboards when she heard Rufus's key in the door followed by Jessica's happy chatter.

'You're up, Annie.' Rufus seemed surprised to see her in the kitchen.

Her mouth twisted wryly. 'It is after ten o'clock. I'm sorry I overslept.' Even as she made the apology she was helping Jessica off with her coat. 'I don't usually. I can't remember the last time I—'

'I wasn't criticising,' Rufus cut in gently. 'Merely making an observation. We had a great time at the park, didn't we, Tuppence?' He ruffled Jessica's already windblown hair.

Without Annie. She was starting to feel superfluous. And not a little sorry for herself too, she acknowledged painfully. She loved this man, and his daughter, so much, and one day she would have to leave both of them. Sooner rather than later, if Rufus's determination where Margaret was concerned was anything to go by!

'We had fun.' Jessica grinned in agreement, her cheeks flushed with the exercise.

'You're probably both cold.' Annie was aware that she sounded a little stilted, but she couldn't help that, either; she suddenly felt very uncomfortable in Rufus's company. 'Would you like a hot drink? I promise to only put three teabags in the pot,' she added as an attempt at a joke.

Rufus sat on the stool next to Jessica at the breakfast-bar. 'What about the "one for the pot"?' he teased, seeming to be looking at her rather intently.

Which was probably just her imagination; it only felt as if she had the words 'I love Rufus Diamond' emblazoned across her forehead, it wasn't actually a fact! Rufus couldn't possibly know how she felt about him. And it was up to her to make sure he never did.

'I'm not having a cup of tea,' she answered him dismissively. 'I thought I would just tidy the bedrooms while the two of you drank yours,' she explained. She had left her bedroom so hurriedly this morning she hadn't even taken the time to make her bed! Now seemed as good a time as any to go and do that.

Rufus was still watching her, his eyes narrowed darkly. 'The bedrooms can wait,' he said slowly. 'Anyway, Jess and I have already done ours. Sit down and have a cup of tea with us.' He leant over and dropped another teabag into the pot she was in the process of filling with boiling water.

She didn't want to sit down and drink a cup of tea with him! Actually, being in his presence at the moment just made her more jittery than she had been earlier when she'd realised how she felt about him. She needed time alone to pull herself together...

She shook her head. 'I really would like to go and tidy my bedroom.' She couldn't quite meet Rufus's gaze; it might be the undoing of her fragile control if she did! 'The tea is in the pot ready to be poured, and—'

'We don't want twins, do we?' Rufus told her.

She frowned across at him. 'Twins?' she echoed in a puzzled voice.

He nodded. 'I was always told that the person who made the tea should also be the one to pour it, otherwise one of the two people will have twins!' He met her eyes innocently. 'It's an old wives' tale.'

'I think it's just an excuse for Daddy not to have to pour the tea!' Jessica exclaimed knowingly.

'So do I,' Annie agreed. 'And I don't know any old wives, so I've never heard that particular tale, either,' she told Rufus sceptically.

His mouth twisted ruefully. 'Does that mean I get to pour the tea?'

'I think so,' Annie nodded. 'And I wouldn't leave it too much longer before you do it, either, otherwise it will be stewed.' She walked to the door. 'Oh, by the way…' She turned casually back to Rufus—as casually as she was able to on legs that suddenly seemed to be shaking. 'There's a telephone message for you on the table.' She deliberately made her voice light.

'There is?' He frowned, hurriedly moving to pick up the piece of paper, quickly scanning the message Annie had written there—so quickly that Annie hadn't even had time to make good her escape when he looked up again! 'When did she call?' he demanded.

Annie swallowed hard. 'About half an hour ago.'

'Damn!' He crumpled the piece of paper savagely in his hand. 'I have to go out soon, so could you two girls amuse yourselves for a while?' It was a statement rather than a question, his thoughts already elsewhere.

To see Margaret, Annie guessed heavily. Because she had no doubt that was where he was going. He wasn't going to return the other woman's telephone call at all, but was going to see her in person!

'There's plenty of food in the fridge for lunch,' he assured them.

'I'm sure we'll manage,' Annie told him distantly.

Rufus looked up at her sharply, obviously sensing her coolness. 'What, exactly, did she say?' he asked shrewdly.

Annie deliberately kept her face expressionless. 'Once

she realised that you weren't at home, exactly what I've written down there.' She didn't mention, as he hadn't, who 'she' was, sensing that he didn't want to talk of Margaret in front of Jessica. She had no idea why not, unless he just didn't want a lot of questions from his daughter concerning her previous nanny, but it suited Annie not to mention the other woman too. She was starting to hate Margaret even though she had never even met her!

He nodded, his expression distracted once again. 'Off you go to your room and do whatever it is you need to do while Jess and I drink our tea, and then I'll go out.'

He could hardly wait to be gone, Annie acknowledged miserably as she went slowly to her bedroom. Or, at least, he couldn't wait to see Margaret again...

Annie sat down on the bed once she had made it, battling with feelings of jealousy that she had never known before. She hadn't even been jealous of Davina once she'd realised she was Anthony's fiancée, just disappointed that Anthony seemed to be trapped in an engagement he hadn't the courage to get out of. But she had learnt the real truth of that when Anthony had offered her the role of mistress in his life! Now she pitied Davina more than anything else.

Margaret, however, was a different matter. She had actually sounded nice on the telephone, which made disliking her all the more difficult. And yet Annie was so jealous of Rufus's obvious desire to see the other woman again that she was having trouble breathing.

But she certainly couldn't hide out here in her bedroom indefinitely, would have to go back to the kitchen and take care of Jessica while her father went out. To see Margaret...

Oh, God! She buried her face in her hands as she cried; surely loving someone wasn't supposed to be as painful as this? Laughter and pain... She had never thought of the two emotions in the same context before, but Rufus made her laugh, and at the same time the pain of loving him, when he didn't return the emotion, was unbearable!

What was she going to do?

What could she do? She didn't want to leave Jessica. And in all honesty, even though her love wasn't returned, she didn't want to leave Rufus either! But if Margaret came back into Rufus's life, possibly took over the care of Jessica again as well, then Annie might not have any choice in the matter. But until that time—

'Annie?' Rufus knocked on the bedroom door as he called her name.

She stood up, wiping all sign of tears from her cheeks as she moved to open the bedroom door. 'Yes?' she replied. 'Do you want to go now?'

'As soon as I've changed,' he said, studying her closely. 'Are you feeling any better than you did last night? Because, to be honest, you don't look better,' he told her before she could answer him.

'Thanks!' she returned tartly. 'You really know how to make a woman feel good!' She really had to start behaving more naturally around him, and the best way to do that, she decided, was to return his banter. Margaret wasn't back in this life yet, and until she was... All was fair in love and war, wasn't it...?

'I certainly hope so!' He grinned unabashedly and her cheeks reddened as he neatly turned the comment back to her.

Annie's mouth twisted wryly. 'Don't worry about

Jessica and me,' she told him lightly. 'I'm sure we'll be just fine while you're out.'

He sobered and nodded grimly. 'I shouldn't be long.'

On the surface Annie found she *was* fine as she and Jessica decided to bake some cakes to pass the time. It was only inside where she let her thoughts wander to wonder how Rufus was doing with the other woman...

There weren't half the ingredients they needed to make the cakes, and the finished products looked far from appetising, but the two of them had had a lot of fun making them, which was really the whole point of the exercise.

'The real test is in the tasting,' Annie pressed the young girl.

'Go on, then.' Jessica giggled, looking at the flat, slightly burnt cakes. 'I dare you!'

'You're the youngest,' Annie reminded her, also pulling a face at the unappealing cakes.

'All the more reason why I shouldn't be the one to try them,' Jessica asserted. 'I still have all of my life in front of me!'

Annie looked at Jessica, and then to the cakes, and then back to Jessica again. 'I know!' She put the tray of cakes on the side to cool. 'We'll offer one to your father when he gets home.'

'That's mean.' Jessica giggled again, although she didn't reject the idea.

Perhaps it was. But, in all honesty, Annie couldn't say she was feeling very charitable towards Rufus right at this moment. He—

She turned with a puzzled frown as the apartment door slammed shut with a resounding bang. What on earth—? Who on earth...? It couldn't be Rufus—could it?—he had barely left an hour ago.

Rufus stormed into the kitchen, his expression thunderous as he glared across the room at them both. 'Women!' he pronounced disgustedly. 'They're all illogical, of course,' he said to himself, throwing his jacket over one of the kitchen chairs. 'The only time any of you make any sense is when you're asleep!' He glared at Annie and Jessica again. 'And even then you're all damned enigmas!' He turned sharply on his heel. 'I'll be in my study making a telephone call,' was his parting comment.

And I don't want to be disturbed, he could have added, but didn't. Although his wish to be left alone was all too obvious, even to these two 'damned enigmas'.

'I wonder who's upset him?' Jessica murmured in an awestruck voice. 'I've rarely seen Daddy that angry,' she explained.

Indeed, who had rattled his cage? as Rufus had once asked her!

But Annie didn't need to wonder who or what had annoyed him; he had gone out to see Margaret—it was obvious that meeting was what had upset him. It obviously hadn't gone well.

And, for all that it had made Rufus so angry, Annie couldn't help her own elation that it hadn't!

CHAPTER EIGHT

'I SOMEHOW don't think just now is the time to offer him one of our burnt cakes, do you?' Jessica very wisely threw all of them away in the bin. 'I don't think he's in the mood to see the joke.'

Strangely enough, Rufus's obvious bad humour had brought a return of Annie's good one! Whatever had transpired between him and Margaret, it hadn't gone well. Annie couldn't have been more pleased.

Perhaps that was slightly wicked of her, maybe even more than slightly, but she couldn't help the way she felt. She didn't want him reunited with Margaret. She loved Rufus herself; how could she possibly want that?

'Let's start preparing lunch,' she suggested breezily. 'It looks as if your father will be joining us, after all.'

Although whether or not he would actually feel like eating was another matter!

When Rufus didn't appear back in the kitchen by the time twelve-thirty came round, and lunch was ready, Annie decided to go in search of him.

He was still in his study, didn't appear to have moved as he bade Annie to enter after her knock, sitting back in the chair behind the desk, his feet actually up on the desktop.

Annie's brows rose. 'Comfortable?'

'Moderately,' he snapped, his expression as glowering as it had been when he'd arrived back earlier, his elbows resting on the arms of his brown leather chair, his hands linked together under his chin as he looked at Annie over the top of them.

'Lunch is ready,' she told him cordially.

'I'm not particularly hungry,' he returned, still making no effort to move.

Annie didn't move either, remaining exactly where she was. 'Jessica says it's your favourite.'

His mouth contorted. 'Does she? What, exactly, is it?' he asked uninterestedly.

'Bacon omelette with lots of toast.' It didn't exactly sound exciting to her own ears, but Jessica had insisted it definitely was her father's favourite meal.

It was really too bad if it wasn't; there were provisions in the refrigerator, but they weren't exactly extensive. Obviously Rufus lived very simply when he was here.

'It is my favourite meal.' Rufus swung his legs off the desktop, sitting forward in his chair, the dark gloom that had been emanating from him, and filling the room, dispelled as he grinned at her. 'Jessica is going to make some lucky man a good wife some day,' he told Annie as he stood up to follow her back to the kitchen.

Annie turned as she heard him chuckling softly behind her. 'Is something funny?' she said slowly; she certainly couldn't see any joke.

'Your face just now when I made that remark about Jess.' Laughter danced in the darkness of his eyes. 'Go on, tell me what remark you instinctively wanted to make back.'

She gave him a reproving look. 'You said it just to annoy me!'

'And I succeeded.' He still grinned, his bad humour of a few minutes ago apparently forgotten.

'Okay.' She nodded. 'I thought your remark extremely

chauvinistic. And I'm surprised you don't want more for Jessica,' she added challengingly; two could play at his game!

'That's an interesting comment,' Rufus said. 'You don't think a successful marriage is enough for a woman?'

'Is it enough for a man?' she instantly responded.

He paused at the kitchen door. 'I suggest, as Jessica's lunch will spoil, if we don't soon eat, that we continue this conversation some other time. And no, I'm not avoiding an answer,' he stated at her derisive expression. 'It's just too wide a subject to dispense with in two minutes.'

Annie was already regretting the challenge she had thrown out. Oh, not because she didn't mean what she said, because she did; it was just that she realised now that when Rufus had something on his mind he could be deliberately provocative. She didn't for a moment believe *he* had meant what he'd just said; he was just spoiling for an argument! And if he couldn't get anywhere where Margaret was concerned he was going to argue with someone else—namely Annie!

After claiming he wasn't particularly hungry, he certainly did full justice to the omelette and toast, even asking for more of the latter. His bad temper seemed to have disappeared too as he teased and joked with both of them throughout the meal. Not that Annie was fooled by this for a moment, knowing he would return to their earlier conversation once they were on their own again.

'That was excellent.' Rufus sat back, replete after his meal. 'What more could a man ask for than two women pandering to his every whim?' He looked at Annie as she made them all coffee.

He was still baiting her. But she wasn't about to bite, not this time. 'Coffee.' She smiled at him sweetly as she put the steaming mug down next to him.

His mouth twitched as he easily guessed that she was inwardly seething at his taunting. 'Thank you,' he returned just as politely.

'You know something, Rufus…?' Annie continued to smile at him as she gave Jessica her drink before picking up her own mug of coffee and resuming her seat. 'You have a lousy temper!' she told him pleasantly before calmly sipping her coffee.

He continued to look at her for several stunned seconds, and then he began to laugh, that loud shout of laughter that showed he was enjoying himself. And he wasn't laughing at her this time, but with her.

'You're right, Annie.' He finally sobered enough to be able to speak. 'I do have a lousy temper. But for some reason you seem to be able to get me out of it.' He looked at her consideringly. 'I wonder why that is?'

Her bravado of a few minutes ago vanished as he continued to look at her, his gaze warm. After a few seconds of this Annie began to wish he had stayed angry—he was less dangerous that way! To her peace of mind…

'What are we going to do this afternoon?'

It took Annie a couple of seconds to realise Jessica had asked the question, and then, even when she did realise the little girl had addressed the question to her, she was so flustered by the directness of Rufus's stare that she still couldn't answer her!

Rufus was finally the one to turn to his daughter. 'What would you like to do?'

'Well, judging by the little there is left in the fridge

for us to eat, I think we should all go food shopping,' Jessica told him ruefully.

'I think the two of you should go.' Rufus stood up abruptly, taking some money out of his pocket and putting it down on the breakfast-bar. 'I have some work to do. Take a taxi there and back, and don't overstock; we're probably only going to be here another couple of days.' He paused at the door. 'And don't worry about food for this evening; I'm sure Jessica would be very disappointed if we didn't go to her favourite restaurant for pizza.'

'Thank you, Daddy.' Jessica grinned at him, that familiar grin turning to a giggle once her father had left the room. 'Don't worry Annie.' She laughed at Annie's perplexed expression. 'I'm not sure what was going on between you and Daddy during lunch, but I think he wasn't being very kind to you—and I knew if I said we wanted to go shopping he would run away! You're right, Annie.' She shook her head with affection. 'He does have a bad temper!'

For one so young in years, Jessica was very astute. Rufus hadn't exactly been unkind to her earlier, but he had certainly been spoiling for a fight. And as the only other adult within touching distance she was the most likely candidate. Annie had to admit that without Jessica's calming presence she would probably have been only too happy to be his opponent!

Annie laughed softly, her tension instantly easing. 'Let's go and do that shopping.'

Jessica stood up, her ankle hardly troubling her at all now. 'We could get all the ingredients to make a nice hot curry tomorrow; that should steam Daddy's temper out of him!'

'Now, that isn't nice,' Annie reproved her lightly, but she couldn't help but smile at the thought of Rufus with steam coming out of his ears…

Rufus wasn't in that deliberately provocative mood any more when they went out for dinner later that evening; in fact he barely spoke at all, seeming totally distracted. Annie wasn't sure which was worse—a taunting Rufus or an almost silent one!

'Bad-tempered, and now he's very quiet,' Jessica ruminated as she climbed into bed later. 'I've never, ever seen Daddy be quite like this…'

Annie shrugged dismissively, although she had to admit it hadn't been a very comfortable evening for any of them. 'He obviously has something on his mind.' Or someone! The problem of the elusive Margaret was obviously still with him. But she couldn't exactly tell Jessica that!

In fact, it suited her that Rufus didn't want to discuss Margaret in front of his daughter; feeling about him as she did, it would be too painful for her to talk about his preoccupation with another woman!

'I hope he isn't going to leave again,' Jessica said wistfully, sitting up in bed, her arms wrapped about her knees.

Annie felt her stomach lurch at the thought of it. Rufus go away again… He had been gone for three months the last time!

The thought of not seeing him for another three months made her feel sick. She couldn't imagine not having him around, whether he be teasing or deliberately baiting her. How different were her feelings towards him now from when he had first arrived home—was it only three days ago? Then she had believed herself in love with his brother. How weak and insipid were the emotions she had felt towards Anthony compared to what she now felt for Rufus. She could hardly wait to get away from Anthony yesterday, whereas the mere thought of Rufus leaving made her feel physically ill.

'Do you think he is?' She looked anxiously at Jessica, her lips feeling stiff and unmoving as she spoke.

The young girl shrugged. 'It's difficult to tell,' she sighed. 'When he goes, he just goes.'

Which was probably the real reason why he had brought Annie along this weekend—he couldn't just abandon Jessica here on her own if he was called away suddenly. Annie's heart felt even heavier at this realisation.

She smoothed back Jessica's hair as she settled her down onto the pillows. 'Well, I wouldn't worry about it until it happens,' she soothed—she would do enough worrying about it for both of them! 'Just enjoy the time you do have with him.' As she intended to.

Rufus was sitting in the lounge, staring morosely into the glass of whisky he cradled in his hands, when Annie returned from putting Jessica to bed. He didn't look as if he was in the mood to enjoy anything!

'Jessica is worried about you,' Annie told him bluntly as she stood in the open doorway.

She at once had his attention as he looked across at her. 'Jess is?' He looked troubled.

'Mmm.' Annie moved further into the room. 'She thinks you may be going away again.'

'Well, I'm not,' he said flatly.

'I didn't say you were.' Although she couldn't help

but feel relieved that he wasn't. 'Only that Jessica thinks you are.'

He looked irritated. 'And why should she think that?'

Probably because he hadn't really been here all day! 'I have no idea,' she replied. 'You would have to ask Jessica that.'

'Is this your roundabout way of telling me to go up and reassure Jess?' he ventured.

He obviously wasn't a man who liked to feel he had been manoeuvred into anything! 'I don't use roundabout ways, Rufus,' Annie told him evenly. 'I am merely re-lating to you what Jessica said to me—'

'Okay. Okay!' he bit back impatiently, putting his glass down heavily on the coffee table as he stood up. 'I'm going.' He held up his hands defensively. 'God save me from a woman trying to be reasonable,' he said as he crossed the room to the door. 'It isn't in the nature of the beast,' he added insultingly as he left the room.

He was the one being completely unreasonable. Annie didn't doubt for a moment that she was the recipient of his redirected anger. Rufus was again going out of his way to pick a fight with her, and if this carried on much longer he was going to get one!

'I thought we could have a game of chess.' Annie looked up and smiled at him when he returned a few minutes later.

The chess set was already set up in the corner of the room; she had merely moved the table over so that it stood between the two armchairs.

If Rufus wanted a fight, this was the safest way of having one. Besides, if he was concentrating on the game, then he couldn't sit and brood...

'Unless you have something else to do this evening?'

she added as an afterthought. Although one thing she was sure of: he wasn't going to see Margaret!

'Nothing that can't wait,' he answered as he sat down opposite her. 'Are you any good at this?' he rasped, eyes darkly probing.

'I haven't played for a while.' There hadn't been too much time in between working and taking care of herself.

'Great!' he responded bad-temperedly. 'You had better go first, then.' He hunched over in his seat.

Annie felt the warmth of angry colour in her cheeks. 'It's customary to toss a coin for it,' she said softly.

He opened his mouth to give her another sharp reply, but something in her expression seemed to stop him. He closed his mouth again, sighing deeply. 'I'm being a moody bast—swine aren't I?' he realised self-disgustedly.

'Yes,' she replied without hesitation, grateful to him for changing the word he had been going to use to describe himself.

He chuckled softly, some of the humour returning to his eyes. 'At least you're honest!' He grinned.

She looked across at him defiantly. 'For a woman?'

'God, I have been an insulting swine today, haven't I?' He shook his head. 'Will one apology suffice, or shall I go through each and every one of them?' he cajoled.

Annie couldn't help her lips curving upwards at his remorseful expression. 'Why don't we play the game of chess first—and then see if you still feel like apologising?'

His brows rose. 'Are you that good…?'

She gave him an enigmatic smile in reply. Although, in truth, she was no longer sure how good she was; she hadn't played for such a long time. She wanted to beat him; she knew that.

She won the toss of the coin, and began the game. And for the next half an hour there was barely a word spoken by either of them as they concentrated on their moves. But Annie could tell they were pretty evenly matched.

'You are good,' Rufus murmured appreciatively as Annie took yet another one of his pawns.

'Thank you.' She accepted the compliment for exactly what it was.

He sat back, looking across at her. 'I really am sorry for the way I've been behaving today. 'I just— Look, Annie, you're a woman— Did I say something funny?' He reacted as she gave a choked laugh.

'Not at all.' Her eyes glowed with repressed humour.

'Considering I've thrown every insult at you today that I could think of concerning women!' he acknowledged knowingly.

'Not every insult, surely?' she teased; there were certainly one or two she could think of that he hadn't mentioned.

'All the ones that are relevant to my particular problem. Tell me, why would a woman agree to talk to you on the telephone, but when you turn up in person instead refuse to see you?' His brow furrowed.

Margaret had refused to see him this morning! And he had been stamping around like a bear with a sore head ever since!

Annie raised her shoulders indifferently. 'Any number of reasons.' She moved one of her pieces on the board.

His eyes were narrowed. 'Such as?' He made an answering move.

She looked across at him consideringly. 'Would you be the person this woman refused to see?' she asked—knowing, of course, that he was...

'What the hell does that have to do—? Yes,' he confirmed impatiently as she arched questioning brows.

'Well, in that case, I can think of a very good reason why I would refuse to see you.'

'Yes?' he prompted curtly.

She moved uncomfortably, wondering if she was going too far. But he had asked, and she could only answer him truthfully. 'You're very— You can be—' She stopped awkwardly.

'What?' he snapped. 'What am I?' he looked at her exasperatedly.

She hesitated again. 'You're my employer, Rufus. And I happen to like my job, and—'

'Forget I'm your employer,' he cut in irritably, 'and just answer the question, damn it!'

She had managed to forget he was her employer on several occasions—that wasn't really the issue. 'But can you forget I'm your employee?' she persisted. 'Perhaps it isn't really fair to ask me this question.' She paused. Honesty had its place, but she wasn't sure whether that was between this employer and this employee!

'Forget fair!' he dismissed arrogantly. 'Just tell me why you would refuse to see me.'

She drew in a ragged breath. 'Basically for the very reason you have just demonstrated,' she said carefully.

'I just—?' His brow cleared. 'I forced you to answer me,' he realised slowly.

'Exactly,' she confirmed with relief; she hadn't had to call him a bully, after all! 'If you tried that approach over the telephone, then I could just put the receiver down on you.' Face to face, this man was much more formidable. 'And so, presumably, could this other woman,' she added gently. He still hadn't mentioned it was Margaret from this morning's call that they were talking about, but she knew that it had to be. And it hurt even to have this conversation, his deep need to talk to Jessica's former nanny was so patently obvious.

'She already did,' he growled.

One of the telephone calls he had made when he'd got back this morning...

'She refused to see me when I went to her home,' he admitted. 'And then, when I telephoned her later, she put the receiver down on me.'

'As you've already said yourself, Rufus—' she moved her piece on the board '—your mood has been a little—aggressive today. Check,' she told him with satisfaction. 'And mate.'

'I've felt aggressive because— Did you say checkmate?' He looked astounded, staring down at the chessboard in disbelief at her claim.

It was the expression on his face that made Annie laugh; he had probably never been beaten at chess in his life before—and he had just been thrashed at the game! 'Don't look so surprised, Rufus; a chess set was something the children's home could afford—and there are a lot of rainy days and evenings in sixteen years.' She said the last without rancour. Her childhood in care hadn't been an unhappy one—a little lacking in love, perhaps, but certainly not an unhappy time.

He looked across at her admiringly before looking down at the board once again. 'Well played, Annie,' he told her with genuine warmth. 'You're a worthy opponent.' He nodded appreciatively.

She didn't want to be his opponent, longed for the light-hearted companion from the drive down here, the man who had kissed her...

'Enough of this.' He stood up, moving the chess table back to the corner of the room. 'You're right, I've been a grouch most of the day. I know that isn't what you said,' he acknowledged dryly as she almost protested. 'But I know it's what I've been. Some break away in London you and Jess have had!' he added with self-rebuke. 'Well, that's about to change. If you could pour us both a brandy, I'll light the fire.'

Brandy and a fire... The brandy she didn't particularly like, and a fire...! It was a little too cosy considering she worked for this man.

'It's a little late in the evening for either,' she said, looking pointedly at her wristwatch. 'Especially as I overslept this morning.'

'As far as I'm aware, you haven't had any time off in the last few days. You're here to enjoy yourself, not just to look after Jess.' He sat back on his heels. 'Perhaps you would rather go out and visit friends for the rest of the evening?' he queried with a penetrating look as the thought seemed to occur to him.

It would probably be safer than being cosily ensconced in this room with Rufus!

But a part of her didn't really want to be safe. She had stayed safe all of her life, never causing waves at the home, being easygoing with her three flatmates, undemanding of the few friends she had had over the years. She didn't want to be safe any more—and she knew that with Rufus she most certainly wasn't!

'I'm really not a night person.' She refused the offer to let her go out. 'I'll pour the brandy.' To make sure that hers was considerably smaller than his. She needed to stay completely sober around this man.

He picked up his brandy glass, dimming the lights before moving to sit next to Annie on the sofa. 'There's nothing like a fire,' he told her contentedly. 'The fireplace was the reason I decided to lease this particular apartment.'

She had to admit the fire was lovely—it was also quite seductive sitting here next to the man she loved, watching the flames dance. The few sips of brandy she had taken had warmed her totally.

Rufus relaxed his own head back on the sofa. 'This is nice,' he murmured softly.

'Nice' wasn't quite the way Annie would have described it. She should have gone to bed. Or gone out. Anything else but be sitting here in this dimly lit room with *this* man. Because at this moment she wanted very much to kiss him!

As if sensing that need, Rufus turned to look at her, his eyes very dark, the firelight dancing in their depths. 'The company is pretty good too,' he said huskily.

She felt the warmth in her cheeks—and it had nothing to do with the heat from the fire!

'I mean that, Annie.' He reached out and clasped the hand that didn't hold her brandy glass. 'You aren't a woman who chatters on about nothing. When you do speak, it's because you have something relevant to say. Otherwise you just stay silent.'

He hadn't released her hand!

She knew she should move her hand away, that this was indeed the danger she had been aware of. But she didn't want to be released. She loved this man. And she might never have the chance to be this close to him again.

She arched dark auburn brows. 'You like that in a woman?' she asked playfully.

He smiled. 'I wasn't having another go at women, Annie. I actually like women. What I was trying to say just now—and not making a very good job of it!—was that I particularly like you.'

Annie drew back slightly, but somehow he didn't seem any further away. In fact, he seemed closer than before!

Because he had moved too! He was no longer sitting on the other side of the sofa. He had gently taken the brandy glass from her unresisting fingers to place it on the coffee table beside his own, his face only inches away from hers now.

'Those eyes,' he murmured wonderingly. 'I could drown in them!'

She couldn't breathe! And as his mouth claimed hers she found she didn't want to. All she could do was feel, drowning herself in the passion that surged through her as his mouth hardened on hers, his arms moulding her to the muscular strength of his body, her arms encircling his neck as she drew him closer to her.

His mouth left hers, but only to travel over her cheeks, kissing each of her closed lids in turn, her temple, the lobes of her ears, gently nibbling there as she quivered in reaction, tasting the perfume of her throat before once again claiming her mouth with his own.

She was on fire as she felt his hand caressing her breast, her nipple instantly responding to his touch, hardening, sensitive to his every caress.

Annie groaned low in her throat, melting against him,

her body like liquid fire, her hands clinging feverishly to his shoulders.

She offered no resistance as he lowered her back onto the sofa, her legs becoming entangled with his as he lay down beside her, her blouse open now, smoothed back to her shoulders, Rufus's eyes dark with desire as he looked down at the peach colour of her satin bra, her skin as smooth and silky as that material.

She watched him through half-closed lids as his hands moved slowly over the pertness of her breasts, enjoyed the pleasure she saw in his face, knowing she was the one giving him that pleasure.

As Rufus was giving her pleasure too, his mouth closing over one hardened nipple against the silky material, his tongue caressing in slow, heat-giving strokes, his other hand seeking and finding its twin, touching, feeling her response.

Annie arched up into his pleasure-giving mouth, her hands entangled in his hair as she held him to her, filled with the strangest mixture of emotions, wanting to cradle him to her protectively while at the same time wanting more than the pleasure he was already giving her.

Then the barriers of her blouse and bra were no longer there, and it was flesh against flesh, Rufus's chest naked too, the dark hair there at once silky to the touch, his skin firm and unyielding to her caressing fingertips.

She ran her hands down his muscled back, her nails lightly scratching the dampness of his skin.

'Oh, yes…!' Now it was Rufus's turn to groan, even as the moistness of his mouth claimed one hardened nipple.

Heat. Fire. A longing that made her thighs ache as she moved restlessly against him, his mouth against her breasts no longer enough for either of them—the pulsing of Rufus's thighs against hers told her that.

'I want you, Rufus,' she told him longingly, eyes so dark brown as she looked up at him that it was impossible to distinguish the pupils from the irises. 'I want you!' she repeated achingly.

He stood up to swing her easily up into his arms, his smile tender as he looked down at her. 'My bed is bigger than yours,' he told her. Picking her up, he strode from the room to his bedroom with her still in his arms.

He carried her as if she weighed very little, gently kicking the bedroom door closed behind them before laying her down on the bed, kneeling on the carpeted floor beside her as he slowly removed the rest of her clothes, folding each item carefully before laying it down on the floor beside him.

Annie felt slightly self-conscious as she lay naked before him, but as he began to slowly kiss and caress each slender curve she could see the beauty of her body in his eyes.

'You too, Rufus,' she encouraged tenderly, longing to touch him in the same way.

And when he finally stood naked before her she wasn't disappointed, as she had known she wouldn't be. Rufus was beautiful, his skin tanned, his body all smoothly muscled planes, his waist slender, thighs firmly muscled, long legs covered with the same dark hair as his chest. Naked, with his dark hair long onto his shoulders, he looked like a warrior of old.

And she wanted to be his captive, completely, wanted to know his full possession, and as Rufus lay down on the bed beside her she could feel the promise of that possession leaping against her thighs.

He began to kiss her again, her lips, her breasts, her thighs, making her cry out in wonder and need.

Then her groans of pleasure became whimpers, crying out as pleasure like she had never known before engulfed her, leaving her mindless, lost in a vortex of such scorching pleasure it reached to her fingertips and toes.

She looked up at Rufus in wonder as he moved to lie beside her once again, gently kissing her flushed face. 'I've never—I— Oh, Rufus…!' Her arms moved about his shoulders as she hugged him to her.

He raised his head slowly, his gaze gentle now. 'Have you never made love, Annie?' he asked gruffly. 'Or just never known the pleasure it could give you?'

'Neither!' she choked a little self-consciously. She was such an innocent, had never guessed, never known…!

Rufus's smile deepened. 'Then I'm glad, and honoured, that I'm the first.' He smoothed back the dampness of her hair from her brow, gently brushing her lips with his own. 'Now I think we should get under the covers, cuddle up, and go to sleep.' He stood up, folding back the duvet invitingly.

Annie blinked up at him. 'But you— We haven't— You haven't—'

He knelt on the bed beside her again, lightly touching her heated cheeks. 'I don't have anything with me, Annie. And I doubt very much, in the circumstances, that you do…?' He raised questioning brows, shrugging helplessly as she shook her head. 'I don't want the consequences of our first time together to be something that you spend the next few weeks worrying about.' He settled her under the duvet before climbing into the bed next to her, his arm about her shoulders as he moulded her into him.

Annie didn't doubt for a moment that he had wanted her as much as she had wanted him—had felt his need. And he was denying himself all that because of her innocence...

Her arms moved about him as she held on tightly to him. She loved this man; she knew that without a doubt as his steady breathing lulled them both into a deep sleep.

CHAPTER NINE

ANNIE was totally disorientated when she woke up the next morning and found herself not in Rufus's bed or his arms but back in her own room, in her own bed, and by herself.

Rufus must have carried her here some time during the night or early morning. As she sat up in bed she saw her neatly folded clothes—even her blouse and bra—laid on the bedroom chair.

Jessica...

Rufus had been aware, even if Annie hadn't, that Jessica shouldn't find them snuggled up in bed together this morning. Or some of Annie's clothing scattered about the sitting-room!

She stretched in the bed, her body feeling different somehow, still very much aware of the aching pleasure given by Rufus's hands and lips. Her only regret was that she hadn't known his full possession. But that might still happen.

What would his behaviour towards her be like this morning? Would he be her employer once again? Or would there be the memory of last night in his eyes too? God, she hoped so. Because she would never forget it! She didn't think she could bear it if Rufus chose to ignore the passion they had shared so completely—

'Tea,' Jessica announced brightly as she entered the bedroom after the briefest of knocks. She put the cup down on the bedside table before sitting on the side of

Annie's bed. 'Don't worry, Daddy didn't make it!' She grinned teasingly. 'He's gone out,' she added a little wistfully.

Annie frowned at the bedside clock. She had overslept again, but it was still only eight-thirty. Who on earth had Rufus gone to see so early on a Sunday morning? He certainly didn't strike her as someone who went to church every Sunday morning, regardless.

She sat up to drink her tea, realising as she did so that she was completely naked beneath the covers, pulling the sheet up with her to hide her nudity from Jessica.

'Where did he go?' She kept her voice casually unconcerned between sipping at her tea.

Jessica didn't know. 'He made a phone call, then said he had to go out. He didn't say where. Or when he would be back.'

Margaret...

Somehow Annie knew the other woman was the person Rufus had telephoned and then gone out to see.

She closed her eyes, hiding the pain she knew must be evident in their depths. Maybe she had been mistaken last night; maybe Rufus hadn't drawn back from making love to her because of her innocence; maybe it was the complete opposite: he had been thinking of someone else entirely!

He had gone to Margaret this morning. She knew it as surely as if he had told her so. Oh...!

'Are you all right, Annie?' Jessica sounded worried. 'I didn't wake you up too suddenly, did I?'

It was as well someone had! She had been lying here daydreaming about Rufus, about last night, about the two of them having a possible future together... How stupid. How totally juvenile. Just because a man made love to you, that didn't mean he wanted to spend the rest of his life with you. She should know; it was usually the opposite! Didn't she have her own mother as an example of that? And hadn't Rufus gone to see Margaret this morning…?

She drew in a deep, controlling breath, opening her eyes to smile brightly at Jessica. The last thing she wanted was to alert the child to her inner distress, because if she did Jessica would only tell Rufus—and he would know exactly why she was so upset.

She had to be adult about this. After all, what had really happened between herself and Rufus? For her, everything. But for Rufus, a man of obvious experience, probably very little. She was a conquest, that was all, a willing woman to share his bed. Because the one that he really wanted no longer would!

But all that might have changed by the time he returned, and Annie certainly didn't want him to think last night had been more important to her than it obviously had to him!

'No, you didn't wake me too suddenly,' she assured Jessica warmly, and the little girl's worried face instantly cleared. 'Would you like some pancakes for breakfast?' She knew they were Jessica's favourite, the answer a foregone conclusion. 'Give me ten minutes,' she requested at Jessica's eager nod, 'and I'll come through to the kitchen and make them.' It would also give her the privacy to get out of bed without Jessica seeing her nudity.

'I'll go and get everything out ready for you,' Jessica told her with enthusiasm, getting up from the bed to skip out of the room.

Annie fell back against the pillows as soon as she was

alone, wishing she had the energy—the happiness!—to skip like that. But with morning had come reality in all its harshness, and last night was starting to seem like a dream.

Maybe it had been? Maybe she hadn't woken in Rufus's bed because she had never been there?

But as she got up out of her own bed she knew none of it had been a dream, her nipples slightly tender from Rufus's ministrations, muscles in her thighs that she had never been aware of before aching slightly, her whole body filled with an unaccustomed lethargy. She might wish it had never happened, but it certainly had.

And when Rufus returned she would have to face him with that knowledge firmly imprinted on her body and mind…!

Jessica had eaten her pancakes, while Annie drank two cups of coffee, by the time they heard the apartment door slam, heralding Rufus's return. Annie stiffened when she heard the sound, her back turned towards the kitchen door as she started on her third coffee; she was hoping it might wake her up and give her some courage too. She knew that it hadn't as she heard the kitchen door swing open. Her stomach seemed to drop to the floor, her hand shaking slightly as she carefully put her cup back in its saucer.

'Daddy!' Jessica cried her own pleasure at seeing her father, hopping up and down excitedly, the injury to her ankle almost forgotten now.

Annie didn't move. But she had to. If she didn't, Rufus would surely realise something was wrong. And she really didn't want him to know what last night had meant to her. She had some pride.

She drew in a deep, calming breath, turning slowly, shrinking back on the stool as she saw Rufus's expression. Last night, in the circumstances, was surely regrettable, but it surely wasn't as bad as all that…? Rufus looked—

'How soon can you and Jessica be ready to leave for Clifftop House?' he barked.

Annie was taken aback, both by the coldness of his voice and the question itself. Yesterday he had told them to stock up on food for another couple of days; now it seemed he intended leaving immediately. What had happened between then and now to cause this sudden change of plan?

Last night had happened…

And from Rufus's arrogantly distant expression it wasn't even a subject he cared to discuss, let alone repeat!

'Clifftop?' Jessica was the one to answer in a woebegone voice. 'But, daddy, you said—'

'I know what I said, Jess,' he bit out. 'But—circumstances have changed. We're going back today.'

He didn't so much as glance at Annie as he mentioned those changed circumstances, but she felt the accusation in the words anyway. Obviously going to bed with his daughter's nanny—the second one!—had not been on his agenda.

Well, it hadn't been on hers either—had been the last thing she'd expected to happen this weekend. In the circumstances, she couldn't wait to leave either, could envisage nothing more painful than spending another couple of days here with the two of them trying to be polite to each other, for Jessica's sake.

'Fifteen minutes.' She stiffly answered his original

question, looking in his general direction but her eyes remaining unfocused, the coldness she had seen in his face earlier enough to deter her from looking at him properly.

'Make it half an hour,' he told her in short reply. 'I need a cup of coffee myself before we make the drive back.'

'I'll go and pack,' Annie agreed, making no effort to offer to make his coffee for him; if she didn't get out of this room soon she was going to make a complete fool of herself by bursting into tears!

'Annie?' Rufus reached out to grasp her arm as she would have walked past him out of the room. 'You're very pale.'

Probably because for her, unlike him, last night had been unique. It had been wonderful, magical—falling asleep in his arms like no other comfort she had ever known. And briefly—very briefly!—she had imagined being able to do that for the rest of her life.

How naive. How stupid she had been. Last night hadn't been about for ever. And, far from being considerate of her innocence, Rufus had probably felt like running a mile from her inexperience. He hadn't been being kind at all, had probably lost interest in making love to her the moment he'd realised she was an inexperienced virgin!

'We need to talk—'

'I don't think so,' she replied, much more calmly than she felt, moving slightly so that his hand dropped away from her arm. 'Unless it has to do with going back to Clifftop House?' she added in a businesslike tone; after all, she did work for this man.

'No.' He looked down at her. 'Believe me, Annie, we

do need to talk, and I'm sorry I wasn't here this morning—'

'You obviously had important business to attend to,' she cut in with a warning look in Jessica's direction. The last thing she wanted was for Jessica to realise Rufus was talking about not being in bed beside her when she woke up. That would just be too awful!

'It wasn't business,' he rasped. 'But it was important. It still is. And until I sort it out, one way or another, it has to take priority over everything else. Is that going to be okay with you?' His gaze was suddenly warmly probing now.

And Annie found she couldn't withstand that warmth, her cheeks no longer pale as she wrenched her own eyes away from his, feeling their heat as she recalled all too vividly how Rufus had looked at her last night, how he had touched and caressed her until she almost shattered in his arms.

'Perfectly okay with me,' she told him coolly. 'I'm just an employee, Rufus; I go where you tell me to go.'

Her chin was wrenched up as Rufus forced her to look at him. His gaze moved searchingly over her face now: the brown eyes that couldn't hide the hurt she felt, the slightly dark shadows beneath their depths from the lack of sleep she had known in his arms, the mouth she could only just stop from trembling, tears very close now.

'I don't believe that for a moment, Annie,' he said huskily. 'God, this is all such a damned mess!' He ran an agitated hand through the dark thickness of his hair. 'Can you try to be patient with me until I've sorted it out?'

Until he had sorted out exactly what his feelings were towards Margaret, he meant! Wasn't it enough that he had gone to the other woman this morning? There really was nothing to sort out as far as Annie was concerned; she had loved—still loved!—and had most definitely lost! There was nothing else to say. Because no amount of talking could change that...

Once again she moved away from him. 'We all make mistakes, Rufus,' she told him evenly. 'Let's mark last night down as one.'

'Is that what it was?' he demanded. 'A mistake?'

'Most definitely!' She shuddered as she remembered how utterly stupid she had been. In her naiveté she had believed that if Rufus made love with her everything would turn out right between them, but now she accepted that a man could make love to one woman and actually be in love with another one. A man's emotions didn't necessarily follow the instincts of his body.

Rufus drew back from her, his expression closed now, totally unreadable. 'Jessica, go and help Annie pack anything you want to take with you.'

Jessica pulled a face. 'Does this mean I go back to school tomorrow?'

His expression softened as he looked at his daughter. 'It most certainly does. The way you've been moving around on that ankle the last few days, I think you could run a four-minute mile if you had to!'

'Oh.' She pulled another face.

'Come on, Jessica,' Annie encouraged. 'Just think, you can tell Lucy all about your week when you see her tomorrow.'

'That's true,' she acknowledged grudgingly as she crossed the room to join Annie at the doorway without even the slightest of limps.

It took Annie less than ten minutes to pack the few

things she had brought with her, but Rufus had said half an hour, and so she took that full half-hour, taking advantage of the spare twenty minutes to apply some make-up to her pale cheeks. The end result was quite pleasing—at least she no longer looked ill, the blusher adding a peachy glow to her cheeks.

The disillusionment in her eyes was something else entirely; she couldn't hide that with any amount of make-up!

The drive back to Clifftop House was made in almost complete silence, Jessica once again choosing to fall asleep in the back of the car, Rufus stony-faced and lost in thought, Annie immersed in her own private misery.

It was the longest journey she had ever undertaken, not in miles, but in terms of emotional trauma. She had never been as happy to see the gothic proportions of Clifftop House as they turned into the long driveway— not even on the day she'd first come to work here!

That seemed such a very long time ago now...

So much had happened in that last two months. She had thought she had fallen in love once, only to realise Anthony wasn't the man she thought he was, and then she had really fallen in love, with a man who was everything she thought he was, and more—he was in love with another woman!

She barely waited for Rufus to stop the car in front of the house before getting out onto the gravelled driveway, opening the back door to help Jessica out too.

'You two go inside; I'll bring the bags in.' Rufus stood on the drive too now.

Annie didn't need any persuading to do exactly that, relieved to at last be away from Rufus. It was going to be difficult staying out of his way for the rest of his visit here, but it was what she intended doing whenever possible. If she didn't see him, perhaps this ache for him inside her would go away.

Celia was crossing the entrance hall as Annie and Jessica entered the house, the raising of her already arched blonde brows the only outward sign she gave that she was surprised to see them. 'You're back,' she stated smoothly. 'I didn't expect you back so soon.'

'Rufus has some business to attend to.' Annie was the one to answer her.

'He is with you, I take it?' There was a slight edge to her voice. 'And not still in London?'

'No, I'm here, Celia,' Rufus told her evenly as he entered the house with the bags.

Celia looked at him coldly. 'And which member of staff do you intend to dismiss while you're here this time?'

Rufus's eyes narrowed. 'I take it you're referring to James?'

'I am,' Celia confirmed abruptly.

'Then I'm afraid you have it all wrong, Celia. I didn't dismiss James; he decided it was time for him to retire.'

'Indeed?' She pursed her lips sceptically. 'Rather sudden, wasn't it?'

Rufus sighed. 'It was his own decision,' he repeated flatly. 'He feels Jess's accident was his fault, and after talking to him I'm inclined to agree with him—'

'I think we should go to my sitting-room and discuss this in private,' Celia put in sharply.

Away from her, the listening servant, Annie inwardly surmised. But if, as Rufus said, James had retired because he felt responsible for Jessica's accident—

'James has gone?' Jessica groaned in dismay, turning to her father. 'Daddy—'

'As I've already told your grandmother—' he gave Celia a censorious look for having discussed this in front of Jessica in the first place '—James feels responsible for your accident. He believes that he didn't check your horse was saddled properly—'

'But I should have checked it too,' Jessica wailed in distress. 'You always told me to. And I—'

'Jessica, I think you and I should take our things upstairs,' Annie encouraged gently, 'and leave your father and grandmother to talk in private.'

'But—'

'Then you can telephone Lucy and tell her you'll be back at school tomorrow,' she added lightly at Jessica's rebellious expression. The little girl could be as stubborn as her father when she chose to be!

'All right,' the young girl conceded grudgingly. 'I'll see you later, Daddy,' she added, almost questioningly, as if she had a feeling he might decide to leave after his conversation with her grandmother.

'You will,' he confirmed easily. 'Annie…?' He stopped her halfway up the wide staircase.

She turned slowly, almost dreading what he was going to say to her. She swallowed hard. 'Yes?' Even to her own ears her voice sounded wary.

He smiled, not that mocking grin, or that knowing smile, but with genuine warmth. 'I'll see you later, too,' he told her huskily.

Annie frowned down at him for several long seconds, and then she assented. 'I'll be with Jessica.'

They ascended the rest of the stairs unhindered, and Annie, for one, was glad when they reached Jessica's

bedroom. She could finally breathe normally once again.
It seemed as if she hadn't been able to do so for so long.
Since she woke up this morning, in fact!

What was she going to do? That was the question she
had put off asking herself all day. Even if Rufus went
away again soon, he would eventually come back. And
then she would have to face him all over again. Still
loving him. Because the love she felt for Rufus was like
nothing she had ever experienced before. Or, she was
sure, would ever feel for anyone again. But Rufus was
in love with another woman. A woman who didn't seem
to return his love. What a triangle of misplaced emotions.

'Can I go downstairs and telephone Lucy now?'

She looked up at Jessica with unfocusing eyes, hadn't
even been aware of the fact that the two of them had
unpacked what little Jessica had brought back with her.
But they had, and the little girl now wanted to make that
promised telephone call. But Annie wasn't sure whether
Rufus and Celia would have moved out of the hallway
yet—there had been the light of battle in their eyes!

'Use the telephone in my bedroom,' Annie suggested.
'That way you can talk for as long as you like.'

Jessica was more than happy with this arrangement,
running off to Annie's room to make the call. Leaving
Annie on her own again, which was something she
didn't particularly want. She had time to think then. And
her thoughts were all of Rufus.

Margaret was still in London, so why, if Rufus was
hoping to have the other woman back in his life, had he
rushed them all back here? Maybe he had just wanted
to get her and Jessica off his hands, and despite what he

had said downstairs he would soon be returning to London?

It would make more sense for him to be on his own in the city. Certainly for Annie not to be around. Especially after what had happened between them last night.

Was it really only last night…? It seemed unreal now, almost a dream—or a nightmare! Because that was what all this had now become.

And she couldn't sit here lost in thought in Jessica's bedroom for ever! Everything was once again tidy, and there was nothing in here for her to do. A cup of coffee sounded like a good idea. She could bring a drink back up with her for Jessica, too.

But what if Celia and Rufus were still at the bottom of the stairs?

Of course they weren't; Celia would never have a private conversation with Rufus where one of the servants might overhear them! And, from the angry expressions on both their faces earlier, the conversation between the two Diamonds was going to be very private indeed!

She was right—the area at the bottom of the stairs was empty as she descended, not even the murmur of voices to be heard anywhere in the house—so as least Celia and Rufus weren't actually shouting at each other. They—

'Annie…! Thank God!' An agitated Rufus appeared in the doorway of Celia's private sitting-room. 'Dial Emergency and ask for an ambulance to be sent here as soon as possible!' he told her forcefully, his face pale.

She blinked up at him dazedly. What—? Who—? Surely he and Celia hadn't actually come to blows?

She didn't believe that for a moment; Rufus might be

many things, but she knew without a doubt that he would
never be violent with a woman. So what—?

'Annie, call the damned ambulance!' Rufus repeated
savagely. 'Celia has collapsed. I think it may be a heart
attack!'

CHAPTER TEN

ANNIE didn't need telling again, galvanised into action as she rushed to find the nearest telephone, surprisingly calm as she gave the details of Celia's collapse and exactly where the house was. The operator on the other end of the telephone line assured her an ambulance would be dispatched immediately, and would arrive shortly.

Annie hurried to Celia's sitting-room as soon as the call was ended, finding Rufus bent over her as she lay supine on the sofa, her face looking grey, and suddenly very old, the hauteur all gone, leaving an ageing, vulnerable-looking woman.

'What happened?' Annie prompted softly as she moved to stand beside Rufus.

He didn't look up. 'One minute we were talking—rather heatedly, I admit.' He frowned darkly. 'But then, Celia and I have always talked to each other like that,' he went on harshly. 'But this time she suddenly went that sickly grey colour and collapsed.'

Annie came down on her haunches beside him. 'What were the two of you talking about?'

'Anthony!' Rufus said disgustedly. 'What else?'

She reached out to touch Celia's cheek, finding it clammy, her hands icy cold. 'She loves him very much,' she told Rufus distractedly. 'She's very proud of him.'

'He's a selfish, egotistical, insensitive bastard!' Rufus rasped forcefully.

'He's her son,' Annie reminded him gently. 'And a mother's love forgives most things.'

Rufus straightened abruptly. 'I wouldn't know.'

Annie looked up at him, brown eyes shadowed. 'Neither would I,' she agreed. 'But I'm sure that if I had a child I would be as protective of him as Celia is of Anthony. As you are of Jessica.'

A nerve pulsed in his tightly clenched jaw before he turned away to stand with his back towards her as he stared out of the window.

Annie wondered if he was actually seeing anything out of that window, or if it was just his way of avoiding looking at her and the grey-faced woman on the sofa. The latter, she believed. Whatever anger had possessed Rufus this morning, it was still there. And it was directed towards Anthony...

'The ambulance is here,' Rufus suddenly said, turning back into the room. 'I suggest I go to the hospital with Celia while you stay here with Jessica. And wait for Anthony to return,' he added frostily. 'Apparently he drove Davina back to London early this morning, but will be back later this afternoon.'

His suggestion that he go with Celia made complete sense; Celia was his stepmother, and he was the obvious choice to accompany her. But Annie didn't particularly relish the idea of being the one to wait here for Anthony's return!

But she didn't voice any of her own feelings, standing back as Rufus admitted the paramedics to do their work, feeling rather superfluous as they took over, eventually lifting Celia onto the stretcher and carrying her out to the waiting vehicle, Rufus following closely behind.

And then the ambulance, plus Celia and Rufus, was

gone, and an eerie calm settled over the house. Eerie, because it certainly wasn't restful.

It was left to Annie to break the news to the rest of the household, including Jessica, who, after being buoyant from her chat with Lucy, suddenly became very quiet.

'Is Granny going to die?' Jessica suddenly burst out, her throat moving convulsively as she choked back the tears.

It would be so much easier to say no, she wasn't— and pray that was the truth. But Annie really couldn't do that, had no idea how serious Celia's condition was.

'I don't know, Jessica,' she answered honestly.

'My grandfather died when I was a baby,' Jessica rejoined evenly.

Annie held the little girl's hand tightly. 'I know, darling.'

'My mummy died, too,' Jessica said tightly.

Annie felt her heart contract at the stark truth of Jessica's words; her mother had died and left her. As had Annie's own mother. And Rufus's. Everyone died eventually. That was the one true fact of life that was inevitable.

Her hand tightened around Jessica's. 'Let's hope that Granny will get better.'

Jessica chewed on her bottom lip, still fighting the tears. 'My mummy went out on a boat with Uncle Anthony, and never came back.'

Annie frowned. Joanne and Anthony...? Was this the boating accident Rufus had spoken of the very first afternoon she met him? Joanne—and Anthony?

'That doesn't mean Granny won't come back from the hospital,' she assured Jessica.

'Will I be able to go and see her?' Jessica persisted, suddenly looking very young.

'If your daddy says she's well enough,' Annie answered evasively—because she really didn't know how ill Celia was! 'Let's have a game of chess while we wait to hear from him,' she encouraged as a distraction. 'Your father tells me you play well.'

Jessica gave her a derisive look that reminded Annie so achingly of Rufus. 'Daddy tells me you play even better!'

Annie laughed, relieved to have something to laugh at. 'He wasn't really concentrating last night when we played.' His thoughts had all been with another woman!

'I don't mind losing,' Jessica admitted. 'Daddy says it's good experience.'

'Does he?' Annie returned dryly; she very much doubted Rufus had ever been pleased at the experience of losing!

Jessica giggled at her wry expression. 'I don't think he thought so last night…!' She giggled again. 'I still can't believe you actually beat him.' She shook her head as they set up the chessboard. 'I don't think that's ever happened to him before.'

Annie bent her head over the game as her own smile faded; she didn't think it would ever happen again, either. Because she very much doubted she would spend any more time alone with Rufus…

But she was relieved the suggestion of chess seemed to have taken Jessica's mind off her maudlin thoughts of death. It was sad that Jessica had such tragic memories to carry through life with her. And how awful that her mother had died in such a terrible way. Drowning, fighting for breath and simply taking in water instead of air, was a horrible way for anyone to die.

But at least now she knew Joanne wasn't the one who had committed suicide down in the cove.

Which meant that probably Rufus's mother had...

How awful if two Diamond brides had met their death by drowning.

And now Celia, a third Diamond bride, was seriously ill in hospital—Annie realised she was becoming maudlin herself now, and that wouldn't help anyone!

How quickly she had become caught up in the lives and emotions of this family. But they seemed to be a family dogged by misfortune. Even Anthony was marrying a woman he had no intention of being faithful to. She sincerely hoped Rufus was right, and that this was not a typical example of family life!

She managed to beat Jessica at chess quite easily, although she could see by Jessica's strategy that, as she got older, she would be a force to be reckoned with; no doubt she would have the same determination to win as her father!

'Do you think Daddy will ring us once he knows how Granny is?' Jessica asked once they had cleared the game away.

Obviously Jessica hadn't been distracted by the chess game at all! 'Let's hope so.' She stood up. 'Come on, it's time to go in search of some lunch.' Empty tummies weren't going to help anyone, either.

It was mid-afternoon before the expected call came through from Rufus, and he sounded incredibly weary. 'Celia is awake now,' he said tonelessly. 'It wasn't a heart attack, after all, but she's going to stay on in hospital for a few days anyway. I'm just arranging for a private room for her now,' he told Annie. 'I should be back soon.'

He seemed to be missing a lot out; if it hadn't been a heart attack, why had Celia collapsed in that way? Why were they keeping her in hospital for a few days? Surely twenty-four hours was the normal time for observation?

But Annie was very aware of Jessica hopping from one foot to the other as she stood at Annie's elbow, desperate to know her grandmother wasn't going to die. 'Jessica would like to see Celia,' she told Rufus bluntly, hoping he would realise why Jessica was so anxious to do that; she could hardly explain exactly why, with Jessica standing so close.

'Not today.' Rufus's voice was harsh. 'Maybe tomorrow, when Celia is more—composed.'

He sounded strange, not at all the confident Rufus she was used to. Maybe Celia's collapse had made him realise he did have some affection for his stepmother, after all...

'Could you give Celia Jessica's love?' She smiled as Jessica nodded enthusiastically beside her. 'And my best wishes.'

'I'll do that,' he returned distantly. 'I don't suppose Anthony is back yet?' His voice hardened as he spoke of his brother.

Not yet. And Annie couldn't say she wasn't rather relieved that he wasn't. They hadn't parted on good terms, and she didn't think he would thank her for being the one to pass on the news about his mother, either.

'No,' she answered Rufus evenly.

'Fine,' he rasped. 'I did try telephoning Davina's parents, hoping to catch him there, but apparently he left a couple of hours ago.'

Which meant that Anthony could be back any time now. Annie felt her stomach muscles contract at the thought of seeing him again. The last time they had spoken he had offered her the role of mistress in his life—an offer she had turned down in no uncertain terms.

'Annie?'

She mentally shook herself as she realised Rufus was still talking to her. 'Yes?' she prompted huskily.

'Don't get carried away on a wave of pity for Anthony because his mother isn't well,' Rufus bit out insultingly. 'He's still a first-class bastard. And he always will be.'

Annie bristled resentfully at Rufus's condescending tone. She might have behaved rather stupidly where Anthony was concerned, but she wasn't completely stupid; she now knew exactly what sort of man Anthony was. 'I'll keep your advice in mind,' she told Rufus frostily. 'Was there anything else?'

His answering chuckle was not what she wanted to hear! How dared he laugh at her? Because she had no doubt that was exactly what he was doing. Damn him!

'I'll be back very soon, Annie,' he told her gruffly. 'Keep the bed warm for me!'

Keep the—!

She drew back from the receiver as if it had reached out and struck her, dropping it back into its cradle with a clumsy clatter. How dared he? How could he…? She had been absolutely mortified all day over what had happened between them last night—and he was making a joke out of it!

'Annie? What happened? Why did you ring off so

suddenly?' A stricken-faced Jessica looked up at her worriedly.

She was alarming the little girl with her behaviour, and that would never do. 'Your daddy had to go and sort out a hospital room for your grandmother.' She smiled, smoothing back Jessica's silky fringe from her brow. 'But everything is all right. And your father will be home soon.' Something she now dreaded even more than seeing Anthony again! Rufus was—

'Ah, my two beautiful girls.'

It seemed as if the thought of Anthony had somehow made him appear as he stood tall and handsome in the doorway of the library where Annie and Jessica had settled for the afternoon, his demeanour as charming as ever, appearing to remember nothing of the last, acerbic conversation between himself and Annie as he gave her his most charming smile. He had obviously forgotten that the last thing she had done before going to London with Rufus was threaten to punch him on the nose! Or maybe he was just arrogant enough to think that conversation wasn't important. Or simply foreplay!

'Uncle Anthony!' Jessica stood up to launch herself into his arms. 'I'm so glad you're here.'

'Well, it's nice to know one of you is,' he drawled, giving Annie an enquiring look over Jessica's shoulder as he hugged the little girl.

'Your mother is ill.' She hadn't meant for it to come out quite that bluntly, but somehow it had. 'Rufus is at the hospital with her now, and—'

'Hospital?' Anthony repeated slowly, lowering Jessica to the carpeted floor, his gaze fixed on Annie. 'My mother is in hospital?'

Annie swallowed hard. 'She had a— She collapsed shortly after we returned from London this morning—'

'And exactly where was Rufus when this—collapse occurred?' Anthony interrupted, looking very like his older half-brother at that moment.

'Daddy was talking to Granny—'

'The hell he was!' Anthony exploded angrily, eyes narrowed ominously.

Annie ignored him for the moment, turning to Jessica. 'It's turned a little cold; could you possibly go up to my room and get my jumper off the bed for me?' she encouraged smilingly.

'But—'

'Please, Jessica,' she prompted firmly.

A reluctant but obedient Jessica went off in search of the unwanted cardigan, Annie waiting until the little girl was safely out of earshot before turning back to Anthony. 'Rufus and your mother were talking when she became unwell,' she confirmed evenly. 'Rufus has just rung from the hospital—'

'Which hospital?' Anthony interjected his face taut with tension.

Annie looked confused. 'I have no idea...' she realised dazedly; she simply hadn't thought to ask. 'But your mother is okay; it wasn't a heart attack or anything like that. They're keeping her in for observation for a while—for a few days,' she continued lamely. Rufus had irritated her so much over the telephone that she really hadn't managed to find out any firm facts about Celia's condition. 'Rufus will be back soon...' she finished unhelpfully. A few minutes ago she had been dreading Rufus's return; now she just wished he were already here.

'It would be better for everyone if he never came back here,' Anthony ground out, hands clenched at his sides. 'Every time he comes back he causes trouble. Surely you can see what a trouble-making swine he really is?'

'Jessica is coming back,' Annie warned as she heard the young girl coming down the stairs. 'Please try and remember that he's her father.'

Anthony gave a contemptuous snort. 'Is he?' he jeered. 'Can you be sure of that? Can *he*?' he added sneeringly.

Annie became very still, a look of dawning horror on her features as she realised exactly what he was implying. Anthony and Joanne's affair in London—had it ever stopped, even after the other woman was married to Rufus? Anthony had been the one out on the boat with Joanne when the accident happened. Anthony and Joanne…

She turned to Jessica as she came into the room, taking in the dark, tumbling curls, the deep blue eyes, the face that was so like Rufus's. 'Oh, yes,' she breathed softly in answer to Anthony's scorn. 'He can be sure. And so can I,' she stated with controlled anger. 'I don't think he's the trouble-maker, Anthony; I think you manage that quite well on your own! Now, I suggest you go and telephone the local hospitals and check on your mother's condition for yourself,' she told him firmly, the anger in her eyes that glittered towards him not in the least beautiful, she was sure, before she turned to take her cardigan from Jessica with an appreciative smile.

'I intend to,' Anthony replied crisply, looking at her with assessing eyes. 'Have a good weekend, did you?'

The insult intended in his question was obvious from his tone, and Annie looked at him dispassionately; how had she ever thought this man was attractive? He was like a spoilt child, hitting out without conscience or thought for anyone else's feelings.

'Very good, thank you,' she answered briskly. 'Your mother,' she prompted pointedly as he made no effort to move.

'I'm going,' he assured her. 'But if I were you I wouldn't put too much trust in what happened over the weekend. Much as he may hate it, Rufus and I are more alike than he cares to admit!' And with that last taunting comment he left the room to make his telephone calls.

Annie didn't need that final remark of his explained, knew exactly what Anthony was referring to. Rufus had been involved with Margaret. Was probably still involved with her. But it hadn't stopped him almost making love to her last night.

She closed her eyes to stop the tears from falling. She would survive this. She had survived so many let-downs in her life already, she would survive loving Rufus too.

She had to!

CHAPTER ELEVEN

THE first indication Annie had that Rufus had returned was when she heard the sound of raised voices echoing through the house!

Jessica was in the kitchen helping Mrs Wilson bake a cake, and so Annie had taken advantage of this free hour to sit quietly in the library and read a book, losing herself in a tale of pirates and plunder, transporting herself into the life she was reading about, needing that escapism at this moment.

Until she heard Rufus and Anthony shouting at each other somewhere in the house...

Anthony hadn't even left for the hospital yet, and it seemed unfortunate, for all concerned, that Rufus should have returned before the other man had gone; their argument, as far as Annie could tell, had been going on all their lives, and could surely have waited another few hours!

'And I'm telling you it *is* my business, damn you!' Rufus spoke savagely.

Annie shrank down into the high-backed armchair as she realised the two men had brought their argument into the library where she sat, the slamming of the door indicating they had actually come in here for privacy. And she was sitting in this large armchair that faced away from them, unnoticed by both of them!

What should she do? She couldn't just sit here and listen to the two of them. But if she made them aware of her presence it was highly likely they would both turn on her—that had happened more than once!

'Did you already know?' Rufus's voice was dangerously low now. 'Did Celia know too?' he added almost incredulously.

'It's private family business, Rufus—'

'And I'm the head of this family!' Rufus thundered furiously.

'When you choose to be,' Anthony acknowledged scornfully. 'Which isn't that often!'

'I asked you a question, Anthony.' Rufus's voice was icy cold. 'Did you know Margaret was expecting your child when she left here?'

Annie couldn't hold back her sharp intake of breath, unable to breathe out again in her shock, hands shaking as she desperately tried to hang onto the book she had been reading, knowing that if she hadn't already been sitting down she would probably have fallen down!

Margaret was expecting Anthony's child...!

'Of course I knew,' Anthony answered baldly.

'And Celia,' Rufus persisted softly. 'Did she know too?'

'Yes. Yes, yes, *yes*!' Anthony confirmed impatiently. 'Why do you think she's in such a hurry to bring the wedding forward to Christmas?' he scorned. 'She doesn't want anything to stop my marriage to Davina.'

'And another woman expecting your child would definitely do that,' the other man rasped harshly.

'Margaret is expecting that child because of her own stupidity,' Anthony dismissed uncaringly. '**She** didn't tell me that because of her religion she wasn't using contraceptives. And she won't get rid of the child for the same reason,' he added disgustedly. 'The stupid little fool, was—Aagh!' Anthony's scornful tirade was cut short as the sound of flesh making contact with flesh was heard, quickly followed by the sound of furniture crashing to the floor.

Rufus had hit him! Annie couldn't see what had happened exactly, but she knew anyway. She would have done the same thing herself if she were Rufus; in fact her hands were clenched into fists ready to do so! Margaret was expecting Anthony's child, and to him it was just an inconvenience, something to be got rid of—

'You've knocked one of my teeth out, you bastard!' Anthony said disbelievingly, obviously struggling to get back onto his feet.

'Think yourself lucky it's only one of your teeth!' Rufus ground out savagely. 'What I really want to do is take you apart and then throw away the pieces! You're a disgrace to the Diamond name, and I want you out of this house—'

'You can't do that, Rufus,' the younger man told him with gloating assurance. 'Our father stated quite clearly in his will that, although this house is yours, my mother has the right to live here until she dies—'

'She's dying now, Anthony,' Rufus cut in evenly.

There was complete silence after this announcement, and Annie could only imagine Anthony's shock. She was shocked herself!

'Wh-what did you say?' Anthony sounded as if Rufus had punched him again, but emotionally this time, not physically.

'Celia is dying, Anthony,' Rufus told him gruffly. 'She has terminal cancer. She's known for some time. And that's the reason she's trying to rush your wedding. She wants to see you safely married before she dies.'

'But—I— You— I don't believe you, Rufus,'
Anthony denied, but there was an edge of uncertainty to
his voice.

'You don't have to believe me,' Rufus told him wearily. 'Celia intends telling you herself when you get to
the hospital.'

There was silence after that last heavy statement, and
Annie could only guess at Anthony's bewilderment. He
was almost completely selfish; his mother was probably
the only other person he had any genuine affection for.

Celia was dying... No wonder Anthony was having
trouble accepting it as fact; Annie had trouble believing
it herself. In fact, there was a lot about the conversation
she had overheard that seemed totally unreal. Although
it also answered a lot of unasked questions...

'It's the truth, Anthony,' Rufus said quietly.

'I have to go to her,' Anthony muttered distractedly.

'She's expecting you,' Rufus agreed.

There was the sound of the other man walking to the
door, but he paused before opening it. 'I'm not sure how
you found out about Margaret and the baby,' Anthony
bit out angrily. 'But it's still none of your damned business!'

'Someone will have to support her while she brings
up your child,' Rufus told him bluntly. 'And I meant
what I said earlier, Anthony; you can continue to visit
your mother here until she dies—and after that I don't
ever want to see you again.'

'Once I'm married to Davina, and to all the Adamses'
money, I won't need to come here again!' Anthony announced triumphantly, closing the door behind him as
he left.

Annie sat very still in the chair, torn between a need
to go and comfort Rufus and a fear of incurring his dis-

pleasure at knowing she had overheard this very private conversation between the two brothers.

Anthony was everything she had come to believe him to be—and worse. He didn't give a damn about the fact that his relationship with Margaret was to produce a child. And how Rufus must be hurting to know that Margaret, too, had betrayed him with Anthony! No wonder he—

'You can come out now,' Rufus said softly.

Annie froze. Not that she had moved since the two men had first come into the room, but with Anthony's departure Rufus had to be talking to her. He knew she was sitting in this wing-backed armchair! How long had he known…?

'Since we first came into the room, Annie,' Rufus told her dryly, easily able to guess at her panicked thoughts as she still made no attempt to show herself. 'I would know that perfume of yours anywhere. Besides, I saw your hair over the top of the chair before you sank down into it!' he teased, although he sounded incredibly weary too.

He had known she was here from the first! And she couldn't even begin to work out why he hadn't exposed her…

She straightened, standing up slowly, putting the book down carefully on the table before turning to face Rufus, her eyes widening in shock as she saw how haggard he looked, how utterly exhausted as he sat in one of the armchairs. Not at all like the arrogantly confident man she had come to expect. Although, in the circumstances, that wasn't surprising!

'It's been a tough day,' he acknowledged as he ran a

hand through the already rumpled darkness of his hair. 'What did you make of all that?' he prompted.

She smoothed her hands self-consciously down her denim-clad thighs, taking her time answering him. 'I— It's a bit of a mess, isn't it?' she finally stated ruefully.

Rufus continued to look at her for several long seconds, then his mouth began to twitch, until finally he gave one of those shouts of laughter Annie had grown to love. She was glad she could make him laugh, even unintentionally; he certainly had little to laugh at at the moment.

'"A bit of a mess",' he finally repeated with an agreeing nod, his mouth still smiling, although his eyes were once again grave.

Annie crossed the room to sit on the carpet at his feet. 'But not an insurmountable one.' She laid a comforting hand on his knee. 'Margaret may be having a baby, but think how much worse off she would be if Anthony had actually offered to marry her—and she had said yes!' She looked up at Rufus anxiously, knowing how much he must be hurting inside.

'God, yes!' He ran his hand over tired eyes. 'The poor girl may have made a mistake, but she doesn't deserve that fate!'

Annie tried to smile at his attempt at humour, but her smile didn't quite work either. She loved this man—and she was trying to help comfort him over his love for another woman. God, it hurt!

'There's usually a silver lining to every situation,' she told him shakily.

He dropped his head, frowning down at her. 'And what's yours?' he prompted huskily.

She swallowed hard, unable to think of one at the

moment. She loved someone who didn't love her, and whether he stayed or left she was going to continue loving him for a very long time.

Rufus reached out to gently touch the hair at her temple. 'I'm sorry you had to hear about Margaret in the way that you did, but in all honesty I don't know if I would ever have been able to tell you any other way. I couldn't have hurt you with that knowledge.'

She blinked back the sudden tears, swallowing hard again. 'It isn't your fault, Rufus,' she said tremulously, his very gentleness almost her undoing. 'Besides, I already knew about Margaret.'

'You knew she was pregnant?'

'Oh, no, not that.' She firmly shook her head. 'But I knew how you felt about her.'

'How I—?' He sat forward in his chair, grasping the tops of her arms as he did so. 'Annie, what are you talking about?'

She pulled away, getting to her feet, unable to be that close to him without totally giving herself away. After all, she had some pride. Not a lot, she admitted, because she had still almost made love with Rufus knowing how he felt about the other woman. But she had hoped—had wanted—

'It's very sad about Celia,' she told him evasively.

So much made sense about the other woman's behaviour now—the extra rest she had seemed to be taking, the fact that she was even thinner now than when Annie had come here two months ago, and this driving need she had to see Anthony married to Davina. The latter probably wasn't just because of Margaret and the baby, was also partly because she had known Rufus and

Anthony would probably end up killing each other if they lived here together once she was gone!

'It is sad about Celia,' Rufus agreed slowly. 'It wasn't until the doctor told me this afternoon what was going on that I realised I actually have feelings for the woman, that the thought of her dying is actually painful for me.' He looked sad at the knowledge.

'I'm glad,' Annie said with feeling.

'So am I,' he admitted throatily. 'I've spent so long blaming her for taking my mother's place that I actually didn't realise I cared for her I—I told her that today,' he added gruffly.

'I'm glad about that too,' Annie told him warmly. Celia might have her faults, but she did genuinely care about the Diamond family; of that Annie had no doubts.

'Mmm,' Rufus concurred. 'We talked today as we probably never have before. She—she told me something I never knew.' His voice was so husky now, it was barely audible. 'My mother suffered severe post-natal depression after I was born. They don't really know how to deal with that now, but thirty-nine years ago there was no help for her! I— It was during one of these bouts of depression that she went down to the cove and killed herself.' He shook his head. 'I never knew any of that,' he groaned. 'My father never told me. And I have to admit that—all these years, I've been drawing my own conclusions.'

Probably that his father had been involved with Celia before his wife died; Rufus had been so bitter about Celia's marriage to his father, and the birth of Anthony, that it was a natural assumption for him to have made. Even if it was wrong.

And it was Rufus's mother who had committed suicide in the cove...

'I'm sure your father tried to protect you, didn't want you, an innocent child, to feel in the least responsible for what happened to your mother,' Annie reasoned. 'Post-natal depression can happen to anyone, and it certainly isn't the baby's fault.'

Rufus looked at her with pained eyes. 'You're very wise for someone so young,' he said achingly. 'He and Celia discussed it, apparently, and that's exactly what they decided. And, to give Celia her due, she's kept that secret all these years. It would have been better, for everyone probably, if she hadn't.' He looked pained at all the time he had spent hating a woman who had actually tried to protect him in the only way she could.

It was a tragedy, Annie agreed with that, but there was still time for Rufus and Celia to come to some sort of understanding. In fact, she was sure they were already well on the way to doing exactly that...

'Now—' Rufus straightened '—I want to know what you've been thinking about my—now, what was it you said?—my feelings for Margaret.'

She should have known he wouldn't dismiss that subject as easily as he had seemed to. But couldn't he see how much this was hurting her? Obviously not, because he just looked totally baffled.

She began to pace in front of the unlit fireplace. 'You were upset when you came back here and found she had gone—'

'I already knew she had gone,' Rufus interjected. 'There was a letter from her waiting for me at the newspaper offices when I got back last week.'

Annie shot him an irritated look before resuming her

pacing. 'You were desperate to know why she had left—'

'I wasn't desperate, just interested.' Once again Rufus cut in.

'You were very *interested* in why Margaret had left here so suddenly,' Annie corrected forcefully. 'You took Jessica and me to London with you this weekend because—'

'Why, Annie?' he said slowly. 'Why do you think I took the two of you with me?'

'Because you didn't want to leave Jessica here—'

'It was partly that,' he acknowledged fiercely. 'God, when I came back this time and found out that she had been involved in an accident it took me back five years, to when Joanne died. She was out on a boat with Anthony that day; did you know that?' He looked at her intensely.

She nodded. 'Jessica told me.' But she had no intention of telling him what Anthony had implied. The woman was dead; raking up old grievances couldn't help anyone now.

Rufus gave a regretful smile. 'Anthony doesn't behave too well as a lover scorned. Although if you've heard Anthony's version of what happened I'm sure it doesn't show him in that light?' He sighed as Annie shook her head. 'He and Joanne were involved before our marriage, and it was a relationship Anthony tried to revive once she was married to me. Our marriage was never the love of the century, but Joanne drew the line at having an affair with my brother. Anthony was furious,' he recalled grimly. 'I've never been a hundred per cent sure her accidental death was exactly that, and then when Jess had her fall…!'

Annie stared at him in horror. He couldn't think—didn't believe Anthony—

'I've given him the benefit of the doubt all these years, but Joanne was an excellent swimmer, and Anthony hated water, has done since we were children, which was why his story about not being able to save Joanne when she fell overboard was always believed.' He raised his shoulders fatalistically. 'And for years I've accepted that as the truth. But I have to admit I was shaken when you told me Jessica had fallen from her horse; she's as good a horsewoman as her mother was a swimmer.'

'You thought Anthony had tried to harm her...' Annie realised the horrifying truth of why he had been so shaken by Jessica's accident.

'Only for a short time,' Rufus acknowledged. 'James feels it was his fault. He's started forgetting things lately, and he admitted to me that he really couldn't remember even putting Jessica's saddle on her horse, let alone whether or not it was fastened properly. I know Jessica is upset that he's gone, but it really was his own decision.'

A wise one, in the circumstances. And Jessica would understand that when it was explained to her properly.

As Annie now understood that Anthony's story about his relationship with Joanne was all a figment of Anthony's vindictive mind. She didn't doubt for a moment that Rufus's side of things was the truth, remembered how Anthony had turned on her when he'd sensed she was becoming attracted to his brother...! She agreed with Rufus: the further Anthony stayed from this family in future the better.

'Now,' Rufus said firmly, 'I want to know exactly

why you think I'm in love with Margaret. You do think that, don't you?' He searched her face with his eyes.

Annie couldn't meet his gaze. 'She was the woman you talked about, the one who would speak to you on the telephone but wouldn't meet you.'

'She was,' he concurred. 'And I finally realised one very good reason why she wouldn't actually meet me.'

'Because of her relationship with Anthony?' Annie realised.

'Yes!' he rasped. 'Indirectly.'

'Indirectly?' Annie echoed in a puzzled voice. 'I don't understand.' And she didn't. Surely it was perfectly straightforward; in Rufus's absence Margaret had begun an affair with his brother.

Rufus stood up too now. 'I have a feeling you aren't going to like it once you do understand,' he admitted grudgingly.

She didn't like this conversation at all, hated discussing his feelings for another woman. And Rufus seemed aware of that now. Did he also realise it was because she was in love with him? It would be too humiliating if he did.

'You may as well tell me,' she sighed.

He drew in a deep breath. 'Last night, when we were making love—'

'Do you have to bring that into this?' she burst in tremulously, her cheeks red and burning. Was she to be left no pride?

'I told you you wouldn't like it,' Rufus reminded her.

'Is it necessary?' she said agitatedly.

'If you want to know about Margaret, and why she wouldn't see me, then I'm afraid it is, yes.'

'Oh, very well,' Annie agreed uncomfortably. 'If you must.'

Rufus reached out to put his hand beneath her chin, lifting her face up so that he could look into her eyes again. 'Do you wish last night had never happened?'

'Yes! No. No…!' she admitted with a self-conscious groan. Last night might be all she ever had with the man she loved.

'I'm glad about that,' Rufus said with relief.

Annie looked up at him with wide brown eyes. 'You are?' she said uncertainly.

'Oh, Annie, of course I am.' He reached out and folded her into his arms. 'Haven't you realised yet that I love every infuriating, tantalising inch of you, that the main reason I took you and Jess to London with me was because I didn't want to be away from you, not even for a few days?' he added indulgently.

She was hearing things. She had to be. Rufus couldn't really have just told her that he loved her. He just couldn't have done. Could he…?

CHAPTER TWELVE

'ANNIE?' Rufus raised her chin once more with gentle fingers, but this time she wasn't able to look at him. 'I love you, Annie Fletcher,' he whispered. 'And it's been a long time since I said that to anyone other than Jess.'

Annie stared at him. She couldn't seem to do anything else. He had said it again! 'But—I—Margaret...!' she groaned desperately.

Rufus shook his head, smiling. 'After what you've just said to me, I have a fair idea of the thoughts that have been running around in your beautiful head, although for the life of me I can't imagine where you got them from. Margaret was Jess's nanny to me, nothing more.'

'But—'

'Nothing else, Annie. Ever,' he insisted firmly. 'I'm not saying I've been celibate during the five years since Joanne died, but there haven't been that many women either, and Margaret certainly wasn't one of them. No, I've been waiting for a little red-haired witch who makes me laugh and want her all at the same time.' He smiled at her in a way he never had before, the love he talked about shining in the dark depths of his eyes. 'I love you, Annie. I want to marry you, have children with you. I'm sorry I don't have a better family to offer you.' He grimaced with feeling. 'But they're the only family I have. And eventually we'll have children of our own, and then—'

'You want to marry me?' She couldn't believe he was saying these things to her.

'I insist on it,' he told her sternly. 'After all, you've compromised my reputation by sharing my bed.'

'Compromised your—!' Annie broke off, chuckling at the ridiculousness of what he was saying.

'It won't be so bad, Annie.' His arms tightened about her once again. 'I intend staying around in future. It's time I stopped all the travelling. And, in truth the only reason I've done it for so long is because I couldn't stand being in this house. But if you're going to be here I don't want to go away. I'm going to write a book, Annie. It's been floating around in my head for years now, but the thought of staying in one place long enough to write it has never appealed before. Now it does.' He drew back slightly to look down at her. 'But you aren't saying anything now,' he said uncertainly. 'Tell me if I'm going too fast, or assuming too much. Don't let me carry on like a drivelling idiot if this isn't what you want too, if it's Anthony you love after all.'

To be married to Rufus. To be with him and Jessica always. To have children of their own...!

'Oh, Rufus...!' She sank weakly against him. 'I don't love Anthony—I never did,' she said with certainty. 'I would very much like to marry you. I love you, too. And I can't imagine anything more wonderful than being with you for ever.' She clung to him so strongly now, it made her arms ache.

His breath left him in a deep sigh of relief. 'Thank God for that!' he groaned. 'You had me worried for a moment. But I couldn't imagine your having let last night happen at all if you didn't love me.'

'I wouldn't have,' she agreed.

Rufus bent his head to kiss her, and it was some time later, with Annie sitting on his knee in one of the armchairs, that they resumed their conversation about Margaret.

'Do you remember why we didn't completely make love last night?' Rufus looked at her with teasing eyes as she blushed. 'I'm glad we didn't, Annie. Our first night together will be our wedding night. The way it should be. The way you deserve it to be.'

'Margaret,' she prompted pointedly, before they became side-tracked once again.

'It was the conversation we had last night that made me realise a very good reason why Margaret wouldn't actually meet me in person. She's five months pregnant, Annie,' he said flatly. 'And it shows.'

Rufus didn't love the other woman, he never had; he had just wanted to know, especially after she had written to him telling him she had left, exactly why she had done so.

'We'll have to help her, Rufus,' Annie told him. 'That child is your niece or nephew.'

'We'll help her, Annie,' he assured her.

And she knew that they would. She also knew that they would care for Celia until she didn't need caring for any longer.

As the years passed the two of them would grow closer, and Rufus would be able to talk to her about his childhood, his father, the mother he couldn't even remember, and his never-the-love-of-the-century marriage. And she would be able to tell him about her loneliness as a child, the children's home, the feeling of never belonging.

Because she belonged now. Belonged with and to Rufus.

How different her life was going to be. She would be a dearly loved, and loving, Diamond bride.

'It's bad luck, you know,' Annie scolded affectionately.

Rufus lifted his head from the soft cushion of her satin-covered breasts, grinning down at her. 'Another one of those old wives' tales? The one concerning twins didn't come true!'

'Not yet,' Annie warned. 'But that's probably because we haven't fully made love yet,' she reminded him with a self-conscious blush.

'But we will. Very soon,' he promised, resting on his elbows as he looked down at her. 'The thought of you having even one of my children does the nicest things to my body,' he murmured, moving closer to her as he began to kiss her.

Annie could feel exactly what nice things it did to his body, groaning low in her throat with the same longing.

The last three months had been the happiest Annie had ever known, loving and being loved by Rufus.

Jessica couldn't have been more pleased when told that Annie was going to be her new mother, eyes agog at this very satisfactory answer to her prayer!

It had been a time of talking, laughing, sharing, discovering—their love for each other deepening as each day passed.

And today was their wedding day…

And Rufus, after flatly refusing Celia's suggestion that he spend the night at a hotel, had brought Annie a cup of coffee up to her bedroom half an hour ago—and hadn't left again!

His eyes were almost black now as he raised his head to look at her. 'Annie, I—' He broke off as a knock sounded gently on the bedroom door.

'Annie, are you awake?' Celia called softly. 'It's time to start getting ready.'

'Oh, hell,' Rufus said to himself and he sprang up from the bed, his unbuttoned shirt slightly crumpled, his hair ruffled from Annie's caressing fingers. 'Celia is sure to know the same old wives' tale!' He scowled at the lecture he was probably about to receive.

'Rufus?' Celia prompted suspiciously. 'Rufus, are you in there?' she added sharply.

Annie lay back on the pillows, laughing softly at Rufus's hunted expression. 'Come in, Celia,' she invited lightly, receiving a glare from Rufus for her pains.

'I thought I heard your voice,' Celia scolded Rufus once she was inside the bedroom. 'Don't you know that it's unlucky to see the bride before the church service on your wedding day?' She looked disapprovingly across at him.

'You see.' Rufus turned to Annie. 'I told you she would know that one, too!' He shook his head. 'It's a lot of nonsense. The Diamond brides aren't known for their luck anyway.' He frowned. 'I almost didn't ask Annie to marry me for that very reason.'

'Now that is a lot of nonsense,' Celia told him briskly, coming further into the bedroom, still extremely fragile to look at, although at the moment her condition seemed not to have deteriorated any further. 'I've already explained to you about your mother's death, and Joanne's death was just an unfortunate accident. Besides, Rufus, I was a Diamond bride, and, despite what you may have thought to the contrary, David and I had thirty happy years together!'

Annie had watched with pleasure, over the last three months, as these two stubborn Diamonds had become quite good friends. And Celia certainly couldn't have been more helpful concerning the wedding arrangements, helping Annie shop for her dress and Jessica's bridesmaid's dress, the little girl absolutely thrilled at being asked to be her only attendant.

Anthony and Davina's wedding had taken place almost a month ago, Anthony continuing to visit his mother here, albeit keeping well away from Rufus and Annie. Anthony's plans to make those visits alone were neatly foiled by Davina, as she continued to accompany him every time he came. In fact, Davina's helpless-little-girl act—and the breathless voice, much to Rufus's amusement—seemed to have vanished overnight, and in her place was a woman even more domineering than Celia had been. Anthony had met his match where he'd least expected it!

And Anthony's ceremony neatly out of the way, his future very definitely decided, Celia had turned all her attention to Rufus and Annie's wedding. In all honesty, Annie had been grateful for her help, had come to realise, over the last few months, that a lot of Celia's imperious manner was, in fact, a barrier put up to protect herself from being hurt. The past having finally been put to rest, that barrier was no longer necessary, and as a surrogate mother to Rufus, and indeed Annie, Celia had proved more than capable. They were all going to miss her when the time came for them to say goodbye.

'I'm sure you did.' Rufus gently squeezed Celia's shoulder. 'Just as I'm sure Annie and I are going to have

many happy years together.' He turned to her, his love
for her blazing in the dark blue of his eyes.

Annie was sure they were too, the last three months
spent with Rufus more than enough to reassure her of
their future happiness together.

She couldn't possibly have guessed how it would turn
out when she'd decided to work as part of a family—
but she really was part of a family now. She and Rufus
were their own family, with Jessica and Celia drawn into
that loving fold.

The Diamond bride was to become the Diamond wife
and mother.

Utter and complete happiness.

For ever.

HARLEQUIN PRESENTS®

How could any family be complete without a nineties nanny?

...as a friend, as a parent or even as a partner...

A compelling new series from our bestselling authors about nannies whose talents extend way beyond looking after the children:

July 1998—THE DIAMOND BRIDE
by Carole Mortimer (#1966)

August 1998—INHERITED: ONE NANNY
by Emma Darcy (#1972)

September 1998—THE NANNY AFFAIR
by Robyn Donald (#1980)

P.S. Remember, nanny knows best when it comes to falling in love!

Available wherever Harlequin books are sold.

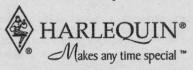

HARLEQUIN®
Makes any time special ™

Take 2 bestselling love stories FREE

Plus get a FREE surprise gift!

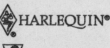
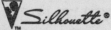

Big, brash and brazen...

THE AUSTRALIANS

Stories of romance Australian-style guaranteed to
fulfill that sense of adventure!

This August, look for
Heartthrob for Hire
by Miranda Lee

Roy Fitzsimmons had those rugged good looks that women
would die for. So why was he pursuing Kate? Kate Reynolds was
more at home in the boardroom than the bedroom. Then an
overheard telephone conversation gave her some clues. Could
Roy be hiring himself out to lonely women? He *seemed* too
genuine to be a gigolo, but Kate decided to put her theory to the
test and offer to pay Roy to pose as her lover.... But would
he accept?

*The Wonder from Down Under: where spirited women win
the hearts of Australia's most independent men!*

Available August 1998 at your favorite retail outlet.

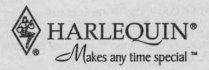

HARLEQUIN®
Makes any time special ™

Coming Next Month

HARLEQUIN PRESENTS®

THE BEST HAS JUST GOTTEN BETTER!

#1971 THE RELUCTANT HUSBAND Lynne Graham
Unbeknown to Frankie, her marriage to Santino had never been annulled—and now he was intending to claim the wedding night they'd never had! But Santino hadn't bargained on falling for Frankie all over again....

#1972 INHERITED: ONE NANNY Emma Darcy
(Nanny Wanted!)
When Beau Prescott heard he'd inherited a nanny with his grandfather's estate, he imagined Margaret Stowe to be a starchy spinster. But she turned out to be a beautiful young woman. Just what situation had he inherited here?

#1973 MARRIAGE ON THE REBOUND Michelle Reid
Rafe Danvers had always acted as if he despised Shaan; he even persuaded his stepbrother to jilt her on her wedding day. Yet suddenly Rafe wanted to proclaim her to the world as his wife—and Shaan wanted to know why....

#1974 TEMPORARY PARENTS Sara Wood
Laura had sworn never to see her ex-lover, Max, again. But cocooned in a cliff-top cottage with him, watching him play daddy to her small niece and nephew, it was all too easy to pretend she and Max were together again....

#1975 MAN ABOUT THE HOUSE Alison Kelly
(Man Talk!)
Brett had decided women were unreliable, and right now he wanted to be single. Or so he thought—until he agreed to house-sit for his mother, and discovered another house-sitter already in residence—the gorgeous Joanna!

#1976 TEMPTING LUCAS Catherine Spencer
Emily longed to tell Lucas about the consequences of their one-night stand eleven years ago, and that she still loved him. But she was determined that if they ever made love again, it would be he who'd come to her....